Praise for *People*

"*People* is a short story collection that will engage and disquiet. Ottone's tales of love, loss, suspense, and the supernatural will not only keep you turning the pages...they may just keep you up at night!"

- Kimberly Poppiti, PhD (St. Joseph's College, NY)

"A creepy and fun collection of stream-of-consciousness horror stories. An interesting read, and I look forward to the next collection."

- Carl Paolino, author of the *Virgin Falls* horror series

People

*A Horror Anthology about Love,
Loss, Life & Things that Go Bump
in the Night*

Robert P. Ottone

Edited by Louis Maurici

Spooky House Press

Scan this QR code for a Spotify playlist
of songs curated by the author:

First Edition

ISBN 978-1-7340445-0-8 paperback
ISBN 978-1-7340445-1-5 hardcover
ISBN 978-1-7340445-2-2 eBook

For dad

Contents

Tell Me I'm Pretty 1

The Veil 55

Bear Hands 67

Cultural Appropriation or Beautiful Love 83

Take Only What You Need 87

The Butcher 91

My Indestructible Friend Steve 99

Kiwi 125

What Would Batman Do? 141

The Dunderbergs 163

The Rainbow Prism 171

Tell Me I'm Pretty

"We'll only be gone for a week, and honestly, you don't even need to be here all that much, just in the morning to feed the dogs and at dinner time, as long as they go out a couple times throughout the day," Davis told me on the phone before he and his wife Kelsey hopped a plane to the Maldives for a family vacation.

"I'm looking at this like a 'staycation,' as the girls of Instagram call it, dude. I'll happily relax at your stately manor for six days," I tell him, feeling genuine excitement building for a week of Palisades living.

Living in Resting Hollow is great and all, but getting to spend some time in the Palisades, the "rich" part of town, will be greatly appreciated. Davis hit it big when an algorithm he wrote ended up part of a bidding war between two search engines. Suffice to say, he made an ocean of money on the deal, married his college girlfriend, and the two are super rich and super happy. Whoever says money doesn't make you happy has no idea what they're talking about. Davis and Kelsey were always fun and a great couple, but now they have a fun and great house to go with the package.

"Where is the Maldives anyway?" I ask, tossing a baseball into the air and catching it, while relaxing in my own meager living space in an apartment complex in the heart of town.

"The Indian Ocean, I believe," Davis says, then, unsure, "Asia?"

"I'll just look it up later, I guess. This was a Kelsey-planned vacation, I assume?"

"You know it. If it was up to me, I'd be smoking cigars and drinking heavily in the hot tub," he says, laughing.

"Also a good plan. I'm sure they have hot tubs in the Maldives, bud."

We chat a little longer, and Davis tells me the house code to get in through the garage, and I write it in my phone. I have off for the week, so spending time in the hot tub, smoking Davis' cigars, and drinking his whiskey, wine, and vodka is at the top of the list.

"Just don't drink all the Blue, otherwise, you're a dead man when I get back," he jokingly warns me.

"Fair enough, dude."

The Palisades are about thirty minutes outside of town, deep into the woods nestled at the base of the Rain King Mountains. This time of year, that confused period between the end of April and beginning of May when the weather doesn't know if it wants to rain all the time, freeze you with wind, or let you soak up the sun with seventy-five degree days and cool nights, results in a perpetual halo of fog around the top of the mountain, around two thousand feet up.

I've never been much for hiking, but I think getting to explore the Rain King this coming week is a pretty neat idea. I've packed my camera, some hiking boots that I bought for a Halloween costume where I was the guy who went hiking and hacked his own arm off to get free when he was trapped by a rock or whatever, and the water bottle that sits on my desk at work that cost me $35 at the sporting goods store in town.

During the drive, I see the Rain King Mountains in the distance getting closer. The halo around its peak. I see the Palisades at the base of the mountain, enormous houses that range anywhere from $700,000 to over a million. Their enormity is somehow slightly diminished by the size of the mountain, but as I pull up to Davis and Kelsey's house, I'm taken aback, as I usually am, at the size of their beautiful home. I hear their dogs barking, and I walk around to the side of the garage. I find the door, which has a small number pad on it. I type the passcode and enter into their weight room.

I make a mental note to lift some weights while I'm staying at their house but know that it probably won't happen. It's cool out, so when I get into the house I'm delighted that it's warm. The dogs jump on me, but they're small. I have no idea what kind of dogs they are, but they look like taller, longer dachshunds. Turing and Iggy. One is named after the so-called "father of computing," Alan Turing, and the other, I wish was named after Iggy Pop, but was apparently named after Iggy Azalea.

I look around the house and realize I've never been here when my friends weren't here, so it's strange not to see Kelsey fluttering around the kitchen, or Davis carrying pool noodles or a volleyball net around. The last time I was here, I was wasted on sangria and singing B-52s on their karaoke machine. Always a good time at Davis and Kelsey's.

I walk upstairs and place my stuff down on the dresser in the guest room. I take my toiletries and unpack them in the shower, and take note of the backyard from my window. The massive pool with a waterfall, diving board, and slide. The basketball court. The putting range. Two grills (*who needs two grills?*). Firepit. Tiki bar. Hot tub. Massive deck.

"This'll do," I say, and start to unpack my clothes.

That night, I relax in the hot tub, smoke one of Davis' cigars, and look up at the mountain. The outdoor speakers are playing a perfect playlist of all my favorite bands, and I'm loving life. The dogs are asleep under the picnic table on the grass, the sky is sprinkled with stars, and the halo around the mountain looms heavy.

***

The next morning, around 7:30 am, I feed the dogs, give them fresh water, and go for a short walk around the neighborhood. When I get back, the dogs are done eating and Iggy is at the back door to the yard, so I let her out and Turing chases after her. They leap around in the grass, playing, while I make myself some breakfast.

While I'm pouring milk into my off-brand Cheerios, I hear the dogs begin barking aggressively outside. Stepping out into the yard, I block the sun and look around for them. I hear them barking, but can't see them. I step off the deck and onto the grass and look deeper into the bushes that surround the property. Eventually, I see Turing, with Iggy slightly behind him, stiff, barking at a section of woods set far back from the property, separated by a thick, heavy duty stockade fence.

The gaps between the posts are barely an inch apart, but Turing sees something.

I walk over to Turing and ask him what's wrong, half expecting him to answer. He goes quiet and I hear the shuffling of brush in the general direction of where Turing was barking. I peek through the fence, but see nothing. The wind picks up a bit, and the trees and bushes sway softly, but I don't see anything that should make the dogs bark like that.

Turing turns and returns to the back door, almost dejected. I remain at the fence a moment longer, before I head back to my breakfast.

After finishing breakfast, I'm in the shower when I think I hear the dogs barking. Turning the water off, I step out of the shower and walk, nude, to the landing overlooking the first floor of the house. "Hello?"

The dogs aren't barking. I don't even hear the jingling of their collars. "Turing? Iggy?"

Nothing. I step back into the guest room, dry myself off, throw on some clothes quickly and head downstairs. Both dogs are lying on the couch, lazily looking out the massive windows into the back yard.

"What's the deal, pups?"

They look at me quizzically. I walk to the window and look outside at the yard. I don't see anything out of the ordinary until I look past the fence into the small park that's next to the house and see a young woman, very pale, wearing one of those hipster-style mini dresses that actresses like Zooey Deschanel wear. She looks out of place, almost out of time.

"Were you barking at her? Why?"

Of course, the dogs don't answer. Just more stares with their wide eyes. I pet them, slide open the door to the back yard and head outside to get a closer look at the woman on the swingset.

As I get closer, I realize the term "woman" doesn't fit. She's young. Possibly a teenager. But there's age to her. I can't quite place how old this person is, but how pale she is, combined with her dark hair, pink lips, and beaming purple eyes disquiets me.

I pretend to check the bushes close to the fence so I can get a better look at her. She's not wearing any shoes. As she swings, the swing itself squeaks when she extends her legs for forward momentum. She never turns to look at me. She might not even know I'm watching her.

Suddenly, I feel like a creep, so I head back toward the house, hearing the squeak of the swings every few seconds. When I get to the sliding door, I notice silence. When I turn and look toward the swingset, the girl is gone, and the swing isn't moving.

***

That afternoon, I decide to walk the foothills leading to the mountain, to get a better idea of what the entire process might entail. I haven't packed a bag or anything, but I'm carrying a water bottle with me. The foothills are beautiful on their own, and are flanked by a thick forest that leads to the backs of the houses in the development. I make note of the mountain, and the trail that ends at the highest point of the foothills. I study it a while, sit down on a large rock at the base of the trail, and start to make notes in a small notebook I brought along.

"Hello."

I look up. It's her. "Hi."

"What're you writing?" She's still not wearing shoes. She's only a few feet from me, but when I look up at her, the sun gets in my eyes. A light floral, almost orange-like citrus scent suddenly hits me.

"I'm taking notes about the trail up the mountain," I say, squinting, the sun in my eyes.

She walks closer, and sits down on the grass next to me. Even this close, I can't tell how old she is. She could be twenty, she could be sixteen, I have no idea.

"You're gonna' go up the mountain?"

I nod. She's staring at me. Those giant purple eyes.

"That's the plan."

I look at her feet. Not a scuff of dirt on them.

"Why are you looking at my feet?" she asks, suddenly.

I shake my head. "I didn't think anyone would go up the foothills barefoot, seems dangerous."

"Not for me," she says, smiling.

I stare at her. The floral/citrus is definitely her. "What perfume is that?"

She shrugs. "Dunno'. Just one I had lyin' around. Why? You like it?"

"It's nice," I say, smiling. I look around to see if anyone else is nearby. The last thing I need is for someone to think I'm harassing this girl.

"There's no one around, silly," she says, giggling. "It's just *us*."

"What are you doing up here?"

She shrugs. "I saw you walking and figured I'd come say hi. I saw you watching me on the swings before. I'm Ebba."

"That's not a name you hear often these days. I'm Leonard."

"Talk about names you don't hear much these days. Are you a grandpa or something?" She laughs again.

"I'm housesitting for my friend, I live in town," I find myself saying.

"And puppysitting, too," she says. She sits cross-legged and I can see her knees and the beginning of her thighs sticking out of her dress. She's so pale, it's almost distracting.

"Yeah, and puppysitting."

She leans back on her elbows and stretches her legs out. "It's beautiful out today, isn't it?"

"Definitely. I don't think I'll start the mountain today, but it's good to plan, you know?"

She nods. "That mountain can be dangerous. Lotta' people died climbing it. Got lost in the woods or took a tumble. That kinda' thing."

"Really?"

Another nod. Her hair dangles in her face and she brushes it back. "Yeah, they tried mining it back in the day, too, but the oxygen just kinda' gets sucked out." To punctuate that last bit, she makes a slurping/sucking noise with her mouth and claps her hands together. She starts ripping and tugging at the grass. Eventually a small dandelion catches her attention and she starts spinning it between her fingers.

I stare at her. "How old are you, Ebba?" For the first time, I notice her ears and the tip of her nose. Her nose flattens at the tip, almost into a perfect square, subtle, barely noticeable. The helix of her ears sharpen to almost a knifepoint. She looks like something out of *Lord of the Rings*.

She's otherworldly. Like from another time and place. But she's here and she's real. There's something intoxicating about her being near and I'm not sure if it's the proximity between myself and her attractiveness or how genuinely strange she is that's drawing me in. I suddenly feel like I'm in seventh grade again, talking to my older sister's cute friends and grasping at what to say to keep them entertained, even when I knew they weren't.

She rises and brushes her dress off. "I gotta' get going. Nice to meet you, Leonard. I'm sure I'll see you around." She extends her hand to shake mine, and we do, then she bops down the foothills toward the development.

***

That night, I'm sitting on the porch, the dogs running around the yard. They dip in and out of the tree-lined border of the property, vanishing from sight for minutes at a time, but I'm lost in thought. The Alexa in the kitchen, which is connected to the sound system wired into every room of the house, is playing a playlist of bands I love, and I'm smoking a cigar and drinking Johnny Walker and thinking about the best way to approach the mountain. Ebba keeps popping into my mind, too, and I get distracted thinking of her on the foothills. Her dress. Her pale skin. Those purple eyes.

Suddenly, I notice that only one of the dogs is visible in the yard.

"Where's Turing?" I say, walking over to Iggy.

I call out for the dog a few times. Nothing. I walk Iggy back into the house and close the sliding door behind me. I grab the leash from the counter and walk into the large yard, as night begins to fall. Using my phone to light the dense treeline, I call out for the dog multiple times. In my pocket are a few treats.

"Come on, ding dong, where are you?"

I walk around to the front of the house and call out for the dog again. The neighborhood is impossibly quiet, and as I walk down the street, I look into as many yards and driveways for the dog as I can. Turing is nowhere to be found.

"Davis is gonna' kill me, man," I say to no one in particular. I listen again. The stillness of the night. The cool air. The dark neighborhood. This is one of those expensive areas where the streetlamps are spaced remarkably far apart and resemble streetlamps from the late 1800's but are powered by electricity instead of whale oil or whatever the hell used to power them.

I walk a little further, turning the corner and heading towards the wooded area that runs behind Davis and Kelsey's house. I shine my phone's light into the woods more, and hold one of the treats in my hand, calling for Turing the entire time. I note, on my way, that many of the neighbors' houses are dark, and notice for the first time how empty the neighborhood truly feels. I've seen neighbors. I've heard their kids playing in their yards, heard their dogs barking and have even waved to them, pretending to live in their amazing neighborhood. But this stillness. This quiet. It's so dramatically different than living in town, where, even though it's not New York City or any busy area, has a significant life to it at night, even for a small town in upstate New York.

"Everything okay, fella'?" I turn and spot a figure behind me, holding a flashlight.

"Sorry, yeah, just looking for my friend's dog." I'm shielding my eyes from the beam of the flashlight.

"Oh, sorry," the figure says, turning the flashlight towards the ground. I walk over to the figure, illuminated by my phone. "Name's Mark. I've seen you around the neighborhood."

Mark's older, in his sixties. I shake his hand. He's walking a Chihuahua. "This is Mark Jr."

I kneel down and pet Mark Jr. "You named your dog after yourself? I dig it."

"You new to the area?"

"House sitting for my buddy and his wife. Davis and Kelsey?"

Mark nods. "Oh yeah, yeah, the internet kid. Yeah, I hearda' him. Pretty wife."

"Sure, yeah, they're good folks. I grew up with Davis. Knew him before he was 'the internet kid,'" I laugh. "I'm looking for their dog, Turing. Got out of the yard. These woods back up to their house."

"Well, that's no good," Mark says. I show him a picture of Turing on my phone. "I'll help you look."

"Thank you so much. Maybe I'll head back the other way, if you look around here? I'll give you my phone number and if you find him, we can meet up or whatever?" Mark and I exchange numbers and I head back the way I came, to the other end of the neighborhood.

When I get to the other end, after about a ten-minute walk or so, I cross the end of the street into a wide open cornfield. Set about a quarter mile from the road, through the field is a farmhouse that looks run down, even in the darkness of the night. A single light is on in an upstairs window.

"Hey." Startled, I jump and see Ebba. She's got Turing by the collar.

"Holy shit, you scared me," I say. "Turing, you jerk, get over here." The dog runs over to me, and immediately goes for the treat in my hand.

"I found him in the field behind my house. I think he was chasing a cat or something," she says. "What a cliché."

"I can't thank you enough. I would've felt awful if I lost this guy while my friends were away."

Ebba's wearing the same outfit from earlier. Still smells like flowers and citrus. "Glad I could help," she says.

"Listen, I owe you one." My phone starts buzzing. It's Mark. "Hey Mark, I found the dog, well, Ebba did, actually. Yeah, she's a lifesaver. Thanks, man!"

"Well, have a good night, Leonard. Keep an eye on that little goofball," she says, smiling.

"Ebba, would you, maybe wanna' come by and hang out? I was thinking of ordering a pizza, and my buddy is basically a functional alcoholic so there's a ton of booze."

She smiles. "I'm not much of a drinker, but I'll come by for a spell."

We walk back to the house, Turing on the leash. When we get there, Iggy is going crazy, barking at Turing, and the two take off deeper into the house, chasing each other.

I take my phone out. "Are you hungry? Is it pizza time?"

Ebba's standing at the entryway to the house, just looking around. "Come in, it's even nicer on the inside," I say, chuckling. Ebba steps into the house. I notice again that she's not wearing shoes.

She looks around the house. The various photos of Davis, Kelsey, their family and our friends. "They've got a really nice life," Ebba says.

I pour myself a glass of whiskey. "Can I offer you anything? You really saved me by finding the dog."

She shrugs and walks to the overstuffed leather chairs in the bar. She sits down. Her feet dangle above the floor, as she tucks herself into the chair. I can't take my eyes off her. "I just wanna' relax a bit. Rest my bones, you know?"

I nod. "There's a …" I clear my throat. "There's a hot tub, if you're interested."

"I've never been in a hot tub before," she says. "How hot is it?"

"I have it set at ninety-nine degrees. So, pretty hot."

"That's like a warm bath. Sounds relaxing," she says, stretching out, her legs dangling over the arm of the chair. I walk over to her.

I shake the cobwebs loose and try not to keep staring at her, but it's almost impossible. "Well, if you're not hungry or anything, we can just hang out, listen to some music, watch TV?"

"Let's just sit a while," she says, putting her hand on my arm. I sit on the windowsill next to her seat and sip my drink. I look at her dangling legs. Her dress. She has her eyes closed and looks like she's falling asleep. Her face relaxes and I watch her chest rise with each breath.

When I finish my whiskey, I place the glass down on the windowsill next to me and her eyes open slowly. "Think I dozed off there."

"Maybe. You looked comfy," I say. She sits up and stretches. I notice a small mark on her neck while she stretches but can't make it out completely.

"I better get home, pops'll be worried," she says.

"Sure, yeah, let me walk you out."

I walk with her to the front door, and open it. She kisses me on the cheek and walks out the door. "I hope I see you tomorrow," she says.

"Me too. Thank you again for finding the dog."

"Goodnight, Leonard," she smiles. "Oh, and I'm older than I look."

"Good to know," I say, chuckling a bit. She steps down the front walkway, onto the street, and into the night.

***

The following morning, I start up the mountain. I've got my supplies, plenty of water, it's warm out, near-perfect conditions to make the trek. As I scale the mountain, navigating the trails with a map I found in a junk drawer in the kitchen, I notice the views of the town, the development below, the cornfield and farmhouse.

It's not supposed to take very long to reach the top of the mountain, but I'm taking my time and soaking in the sights along the way. The amount of wildlife in the woods and around the mountain is astounding, and though it's a cheesy term, I say it with certitude - breathtaking. In the woods, I notice a familiar smell of flowers that I can't place, but continue onward and upward.

When I reach the top, I notice some of the mine shafts Ebba told me about. There's four of them, two of them heavily blocked off by cement blocks and wooden boards, the other two somewhat open, just broken wooden boards in the way. I make my way over to the nearest mine entrance that's not blocked off and look inside. "Hello?"

I hear my voice echo in the cavernous entryway of the mine, and take my phone out, using the flashlight to peer in deeper, regretting that I didn't bring an actual flashlight with me. I walk a few feet and look around, noting the wooden planks put in place ages ago when the mine was first being used. The walls are dark, almost black, and when I run my finger along the walls, it gets covered in what I imagine to be soot or dust. I walk deeper into the mine and hear the faint sound of running water.

Checking the time, I notice I've got plenty of sunlight left to explore the mine a bit, so I venture in further. Eventually, I come to an area that's almost completely collapsed, splintered wood and rocks everywhere. I spot an opening in the rocks and peer through to see if there's anything on the other side. The small opening is just barely big enough for my eye to see, but there's a faint blue-white light on the other side of the collapsed area.

I take out my notebook and jot some notes about the collapse. I also check my compass and note my location. I check it against an app on my phone just to be sure. I take an empty water bottle I have in my bag and place it at the foot of the collapsed rock, as a marker. I peek through the small hole one last time and make out that faint glow again, just to make sure I didn't imagine it.

Turning around, I vow to return the following day.

***

I head into town that evening after heading home to shower after my hike up the mountain. I do some shopping for supplies to dig out the collapsed mine knowing full well that this is probably not a great idea, and when the hardware store clerk asks me what I'm buying this stuff for, I tell him and he stares at me, a look of confusion mixed with concern.

While out, I head to a small coffee shop, and after I place my order, I hear someone calling my name. Turning, I spot Mark, with Mark Jr. in his lap. He's sitting with some other folks, all around his age. I walk over and Mark introduces me to everyone - Carl, Tonya, and Red. Red asks me how I'm liking staying at Davis and Kelsey's house and I tell him it's been great. They ask what I've been up to, and I tell them about the mountain, and the caved-in area of the mine, and the strange discovery I made that morning.

"You sure you wanna' be digging around in a mine like that? You heard the stories, right? The air bein' sucked out and all that?" Red asks.

"Yeah, that girl Ebba told me about it," I say. They all look at each other.

"Ebba?"

"I didn't know who he meant, either. He mentioned her on the phone last night," Mark says.

"She's pretty young. I think she's home from college or something, I dunno," I say.

"Oh, you mean the Simmons girl? Lives down the way from where you're stayin'?"

"I guess so, I don't know her last name."

"Sounds like her. Pretty young thing. Pale?" Mark asks.

I nod. "Yeah, that's her."

"I'd be careful in that mine, kid. Maybe give Mark a call when you get outta' there, that way he'll know if you're stuck under a rock or if the witch got ya' or whatever," Red says, laughing.

"Witch?"

"It's an old wives' tale, like, an urban legend or whatever," Mark says. "The miners, in their digging, disrupted the natural balance of the mountain, and a witch who lived in the mountain cursed them, the mines collapsed, bingo bango, urban legend is born. Truth be told, she was a crazy lady who lived in the mountains, not a witch."

"Technically, every woman was a witch back in those days, if a man said so," Tonya says, laughing.

"I say you're a witch every day and nobody's burned you at the stake yet," Carl says. The table erupts into laughter.

"This town's got a lot of old stories like that, huh?" I ask.

"Every town does, right?" Mark says. "The haunted house at the end of the street, the goblins in the mountain, the witch, the possessed kid, all that kinda' stuff."

I say my goodbyes and duck out of the coffee shop.

***

Back at the house, I pour myself a drink and re-pack my bag for the trek to the mine tomorrow, making sure to bring an actual flashlight this time. The dogs are relaxing in the living room, and I have "Naked and Afraid" on the television to keep them company. Once I'm satisfied that I have enough supplies to start working on the mine, I watch a few videos on YouTube about exploring collapsed mines and how to "safely" navigate them, when I hear a light splash from the back yard.

The dogs hear it, too, and both pop their heads up.

"Relax, pups," I say, walking to the back door. I look toward the pool. Something's moving around, splashing lightly.

I open the door and step out onto the porch, heading toward the pool. When I get to the gate, I see it's Ebba. "Hey," she says.

"Enjoying the pool?"

She smiles. "I didn't think you'd mind."

I shrug. "Scared the hell out of the dogs, I can tell you that."

"Why don't you come in? It's perfect," she glides toward me in the water.

"I'd have to go get my bathing suit."

"What's a bathing suit?" she asks, hopefully kidding. When she's close enough, I see she isn't. I look around and see her dress, crumpled next to the hot tub.

"Ebba, you rascal," I say, finishing my drink and placing the glass on the diving board.

"I'll be a respectful young woman and turn my back while you disrobe, Leonard," she says, with a smile.

I take my shirt off, then my shorts, then boxers. I kick off my sandals and slip into the water. It's warm. She turns around, smiles, and ducks under the water. In the darkness, I have no idea where she's gone. The lights around the pool help, but not much.

Suddenly, she springs out of the water next to me, scaring me half to death. She splashes me and laughs, while I recover. Suddenly, she's on me, kissing me hard, her tiny body sprawling all over mine in the water. Her legs wrap around me and I'm shocked by how strong she is. We kiss for a while, and using my legs, I swim us to the wall, where I can balance myself and continue supporting her weight. I never imagined such a tiny person being so heavy.

"More," she whispers, and we continue kissing. She's forceful. Her hands claw at my back, and I'm worried about her nails digging in too deep and cutting me, but she pulls me in harder, her legs clamping tighter. Pushing her against the wall, I turn to her neck and kiss my way down the nape to her shoulder.

I struggle against how strong she is, her legs tight around me. Pulling her up, I swim us to the steps out of the pool, and walk slowly, carrying her with me as we go, our mouths locked together. I lay her down next to the fire pit and enter her. Her entire body tenses while we make love and she bites at my neck the entire time. At one point, it feels like she nicks me, but we keep going.

***

Later, we're sitting around the fire pit, nude, the flames dancing about six feet into the sky. I've poured us some wine. She curls up in my lap.

"You okay?" she asks.

I look down at her, "Very much so."

"I've never done that in a pool before," she tells me.

"Me neither."

"You don't have to worry about, you know, finishing in me, or whatever," she says. "I can't get pregnant, so, yeah."

"I'm sorry. I just got carried away, just like, caught up in the moment or whatever," I say.

"Little more than a moment," she smiles at me, her face lit up by the fire.

"Will you stay over tonight? I'd love to wake up to that face."

She laughs, "That may be the sweetest thing anyone's ever said to me. I can't, though. My father wouldn't be happy."

"Alright. I'm full of sweet things, by the way. Rot your teeth," I say, kissing her.

She smiles and sits up. She walks over to her dress and slips it on. I watch her tiny body move in the half moonlight and the light from the fire pit. She bops over to me and kisses me again. "Can I see you again tomorrow night?"

I nod. She disappears around the side of the house and into the night.

***

I'm standing at the mouth of the mine, reviewing my charts and checking them against the location app on my phone. When I head inside, I'm looking at the wooden planks holding the mine up. Most look incredibly sturdy and powerful, but some have begun to rot a bit. I know this because of YouTube, of course. I head deeper into the mine, and flip my flashlight on.

Once at the area from the day before, I peer through the slit in the rocks and see that same glowing blue-white light. I take out some tools from my pack and begin to take pieces of the rock down, bit by bit. It takes a while, and it isn't easy work, but I need to know what's on the other side of this fallen debris.

Once I've got more down, the slit is just big enough for my fingers to slip through, so I pop them through and note that the rock on the other side is slick. When I pull my fingers back through, I smell them and note that it's probably water from an underground tributary or something. I continue digging, pausing to take the occasional peek through the slit at the glow on the other side.

I pull the crowbar out of my pack and begin to dislodge a larger rock that's positioned in just a way that if I knock it out of the game, other, smaller rocks might join it. Putting all my weight on the crowbar, I struggle a bit, but feel the rock shifting bit by bit. After about a half hour of trying to get the rock to budge, I take a break for some water.

Listening while taking a sip, I hear the trickling of water coming from the other side of the rockslide. I lean closer to it, listening more. Definitely dripping or light running water. I also pick up a familiar scent on the other side of the rocks. A little musty, but definitely orange or lemon. My spirits bolstered, I go back to trying to pry the larger rock out of the way.

After another forty minutes of rocking the crowbar back and forth, the larger rock gives way, along with about twenty or thirty smaller stones, making the hole through the rockslide larger. I can now fit my entire hand through, and of course, I do. Slippery rock, the sound of dripping water, and a slight breeze, since there's enough room for airflow.

The walls of the other side of the rockslide are blue-white, the source of the glow. From where I am, I guess that it's some kind of moss or bioluminescent fungus. The smell of orange is stronger. I take my phone and snap a few pictures, checking the time as well.

When I exit the mine, the sun blinds me. It's only around noon or so, since I started early, and, covered in sweat, I decide it's best to head back to the house, shower and change, then head into town for lunch. More research into how to make the hole large enough to climb through is needed, too.

***

In town later, I'm walking the dogs and reading articles on how to make the hole in the mine larger, when I spot Ebba windowshopping across the street. She's with a guy, handsome, looks like he's in his twenties. He grabs her arm and the two walk down the street not long after she spots my reflection in the window. She turns and smiles quickly, but she's pulled halfway down the street before I can wave.

I tie the dogs up to a bench outside a bookstore and head inside, both to cool off and to see if they've got anything interesting. The girl behind the counter greets me and asks if I'm looking for anything in particular.

"Maybe something about local folklore, got anything on that?"

"Sure, follow me," and we walk down a row of older books. She points out two on the shelf, both written by the same guy, and tells me about how all the creepy urban legends and stuff I've heard about have probably been written about in these two books.

"The witch, the mountain, all that stuff?"

She nods. "You heard about the mountain, huh? Creepy stuff. The goblins always creep me out the most. Anyway, hope these help."

I thank her, take both books off the shelf and buy them. After the bookstore, I head to the coffee shop, order the largest possible iced latte and sit down outside, the dogs lazily resting at my feet, having been brought a bowl of water by the waiter.

Opening the books, I start reading about the goblins I keep hearing about. The book is as interesting as it is fun, providing the local folklore with the traditional European folklore that most of the urban legends stem from. The goblins, for example, are known as "red caps" and dye their caps with human blood. They also pride themselves on being incredible tricksters, as well as viciously anti-human.

Suddenly, the dogs start barking, and I look up to see Ebba standing opposite me. "Hey," she says.

"You're like Batman, it's scary. How do you sneak up on people like that?"

"It's the no-shoes thing. Helps me sneak around," she says. "May I sit?"

"Sure." She sits down. "Where's that … guy I saw you with before?"

"Guy? You mean my father?"

"Looked awful young to be your dad, Ebba."

"Well, that's who it was," she says, looking away, almost nervously. "He's in good shape. Takes care of himself. Balanced diet and all that."

"Okay," I say. "Are you nervous? You okay?"

"I just, I don't like that you saw him, that's all, he's not very --" she trails off.

"Hey, it's all good. You're still young, you're not supposed to be dating or whatever, I get it," I say to try and help her relax.

"Is what we did 'dating,' Leonard?" she asks, smiling.

"Well, I mean, you know --"

"Relax, I'm teasing you. Can I still come over tonight?"

"We can go out, too, I'd love to take you to dinner," I say. She shakes her head. "Nah, I'm not hungry."

"Well, not now, but maybe later?"

"Maybe. Eight tonight?" she asks.

"Absolutely," I say. She gets up and before she leaves, I touch my hand to her wrist. "You look beautiful, by the way. Didn't want to not tell you."

She smiles. "You weren't kidding about the rotting my teeth with the sweetness thing. I'll see you tonight," she says, kissing me on the cheek.

***

That night, the dogs are out back and Ebba and I are sitting poolside, our feet in the water. I take a puff from my cigar and tell her about the mine. "I was able to move some of the rocks out of the way. Was able to see through the hole to the other side and it was lit up all blue and white. I'd love to show you," I tell her.

"I'd love to see it, Leonard."

"I like how you say my full name. Not many folks do that. Usually it's 'Lenny' or sometimes even 'Len,' which I hate."

She smiles. "Len was that band from the late nineties, right? *Steal my Sunshine*, I think?"

"How do you know that?" I ask, laughing. The dogs start fighting and I rise, heading over to break them up. They scatter to different corners of the yard.

I head back over to Ebba, who's staring at the night sky. I sit down again. "I hope the cigar isn't bothering you."

"No, I like it," she says, kissing me.

She rests her head on my shoulder and we both look at the sky for a long while before I finally break the silence. "I leave here in a few days. I feel like I've seen you every day since getting here."

"You have, silly."

"I'd like to keep seeing you, even after I leave. Is that possible?"

She shrugs. "I don't know. Maybe?"

That stings a little. I guess I was hoping she'd just say yes and we'd keep hanging out and see what came of it, but, I appreciate her honesty. "Alright," I finally say.

She stares at me. "I'm sorry, Leonard, it's just, with my father and everything, it's hard to see anyone, you know? Like, he knows I go out at night and stuff, but I don't really leave town, you know?"

"Yeah, I get it," I say. I kiss her on the cheek and we go back to looking at the stars.

***

That night, she's asleep in my bed, and I wake up and head to the bathroom. Looking in the mirror, I notice a small cut on my neck but figure it had to be from when the rocks slid out of place in the mine. I remember a few rocks catching me in the face.

When I head back into the bedroom, I kiss my way down Ebba's back and she wakes up. We make love again and while lying there, feeling entirely too honest, I tell her that whatever it would take, I'd like to keep seeing her. I also admit that it's probably a little creepy that I say something like that to her after knowing her only a few days, but she smiles and laughs.

"I've heard much creepier things, my dear."

She kisses me and we have sex a third time. The third time is somehow even better than the first and while it's happening, she's gripping me so tight and whispering how she's falling for me in my ear and it's almost like heaven being with her in every way.

***

The next morning, she's gone. I think back to the night before and feel altogether silly for revealing myself so much to someone I've only known a short while. The way things are these days, you're not supposed to fall in love with someone so quickly. The kids call it "catching feelings." Ebba's young, she has to think I'm nuts for feeling this way. Feeling *any* way, really.

I get dressed, and notice the bedroom still smells like her. I check my pack for the mine, and head back out to the mountain after grabbing a banana for breakfast along the way.

Walking into the mine, I see scattered rocks of varying sizes all over. The scent of orange fills the air, almost to the point of feeling like I'm choking on the smell. I notice the blue-white glow more intense down the halls of the mine and when I finally reach the area I was digging out the day before, I'm shocked to find it's been dug out completely.

Standing amid the rock and rubble that was once a solid wall of earth the day before, I look at the luminous area. It's a small spring. The walls seem to pulse with the glow of what I think is the bioluminescent fungus. I touch the walls and scrape some of the blue-white glowing material off, and it continues to pulse and glow on my fingers. The spring runs deeper into the mine, into the mountain.

I walk down a small corridor, following the flowing water and steady myself on the wall. I hear a rush of air in front of me, but when I lift my head, I see nothing. The water just continues onward, deeper into the mountain, into the darkness. I dip my fingers in the water, and it's ice cold. I take my phone out and snap some pictures, then relax next to the spring a moment before deciding to head back to town.

Not sure if it's the shock of being in such a beautiful area of the mine or what the story is, but I start thinking about what could have caused the collapse of the rest of the rock wall. With how far back the rocks were scattered, it doesn't seem like a simple collapse. It almost seems like a team worked overnight to remove the blockage. Either way, I'm glad, and the spring is beautiful.

***

In town, I mention to a few folks about the spring in the mountain, and they say that I should tell the police, but I decide against it. The police won't be super thrilled at the idea of having to up their patrols of the mountain, and, specifically, that mine, so I see no harm in keeping it from them until I take Ebba up there.

I'm having lunch at a diner and looking at the mountain and wondering what other secrets are inside. I think about how excited I am to take Ebba to the spring. I picture us both being rebels and stripping our clothes off to dip in the icy water. I picture her reacting to the chill running up her back, and how desperately I want to see her enjoying the spring.

***

Back at the house, I let the dogs outside and head out to sit by the pool. It's beautiful out, so I take a swim, then grab a cigar, pour a drink, and relax by the pool, music playing over the sound system.

I keep expecting to see Ebba every time I look around. But I never do. The entire day goes by, and I don't see or hear from her. I spend most of the time in the back yard with the dogs, taking breaks from soaking up the sun to get water for them, or to give them treats. I even take the dogs for a couple walks, hoping to see her in the neighborhood, but I don't.

I think maybe she got scared by our conversation the other night, so I try to push her out of my head. Hours go by, but she keeps popping in there, and I feel silly, so I drink even more. Eventually, I fall asleep in a lounge chair, poolside, and when I wake up, it's nighttime.

***

Stumbling up the stairs, still a little drunk, I make my way to the bedroom. The dogs are asleep, and it's time I follow suit.

I fall into the bed, and my mind drifts back to the mine. I think of the glow of the walls, and the chill of the water and when I look toward the window, I see a white face staring back at me. That same blue-white glow of the cave surrounding the face.

I feel a remarkable amount of panic but can't move. The glow has washed over me and I can't take my eyes off the face. I only recognize it as a face based solely on the basic eye placement and slit of a mouth. It certainly doesn't look entirely human. It doesn't look like anything but a glowing orb of blue and white.

My body is too exhausted to react, but my mind, still swimming in whiskey, pieces the face together as Ebba's.

The window opens on its own, and Ebba floats in. She undresses me, slips her dress off, and slides into bed with me. We make love and I tell her how I missed seeing her that day and couldn't wait to show her the mine. She tells me she missed me, too. After a while, we finish, and fall asleep in each other's arms.

***

I wake up alone. Fully clothed. The window is open, and my head is pounding. I walk downstairs, and let the dogs out, preparing their breakfast and putting fresh water in their bowls. I make myself some bacon and eggs, praying that the grease will help the hangover.

The dogs are playing outside while I'm eating and drinking copious amounts of water. I notice my glass from the night before is still by the pool, and make a mental note to grab it later. A knock at the door helps me shake the cobwebs loose and when I answer it, there's no one there.

Just a note:

Meet me at the mine in two hours. I've got something to show you. - Ebba

I pack a small bag, water, some food, and head off to the mountains. Now that I've done the trip a few times, the journey to the mine has gotten a lot easier. When I reach the mouth of the mine, I look around for Ebba, but she's nowhere to be found.

While walking down the corridors of the mine toward the spring and the glow, I move quickly, wanting to see the spring at least one more time before heading back to town when Davis and Kelsey get home tomorrow. I turn a few corners and come to the rocks scattered everywhere and see Ebba waiting at the spring.

"Hey," she says, with a wave. She's not alone. Her dad is with her.

"Hi there," I say, nervous. Her dad looks annoyed at my presence. He eyes me while dipping his fingers in the spring.

"We can't believe you found the spring. Feels like we've been waiting forever for someone to find it," Ebba starts. "Right?"

Her dad looks up at her and nods. "About three centuries or so, yeah."

"Yeah, that's a long time to wait, for sure," I say, not really paying attention. "So, what did you want to show me? Did you want me to meet your father?"

I walk over to him and extend my hand. He eyes me, confused. He looks at Ebba, "Your father?"

Her "dad" starts laughing.

"No, no, look, not that. Leonard, the past few days, for me, have been perfect. Spending time with you. Getting to know you. I've loved every part of it," she starts.

"Look, you don't need to say anything, I've heard it before, and have said it a few times myself, you're not interested, I get it," I start.

She places her finger on my lips to shut me up. "Leonard, just listen. This is Abijah. He's not my father in the way your people think. He's the one who created me, yes, but to us, a father is just the person who brings you into our world. As a male, anyway, a female would be a mother, similar to your people, too."

"What do you mean 'your' people?"

She sighs. Whatever she's trying to tell me is hard for her. "I don't know, I guess I --"

"Just show him, Ebba," Abijah shouts, causing Ebba to jump.

"Hey, man relax. Ebba, whatever you're trying to tell me, you can. I won't be upset or anything," I reassure her, putting my hands on her shoulders.

"Maybe I *should* just show you," she says, taking a few steps back.

The fungus on the walls begins to slowly pulse, rhythmically, building speed. Abijah and I watch as Ebba's body begins to glow the same color as the walls of the mine. The water begins to ripple, as if tiny splashes of water or rocks are dropping into it.

"Ebba ... ?"

I shield my eyes from the glow coming off her body, and wait until the light dims. When I lower my hand, Ebba is standing in the same spot, her features distorted a bit. Her eyes have a sharper angle to them. Her ears come to a point along the top ridge.

She takes a cautious step toward me. "Leonard, this is who I am," she starts. I notice the fangs in her mouth.

"What - ? I don't understand, Ebba, what *are* you?"

"Your kind have a lot of names for what we are," Abijah says. "Two are more common than others, though: fairies or vampires, take your pick."

I walk toward her. "Do you drink blood?"

"Sometimes," she says, quietly. "We can eat normal food, but it messes up our powers if we eat too much."

"Powers?"

"There's a lot. Not all of them like in the stories, but we can fly limited distances," she says.

"Like bees, man," Abijah adds.

She shrugs. She's having a hard time looking me in the eye. "What are you thinking?"

I lift her chin and kiss her. "I think you're pretty great, Ebba."

"That's part of the problem, Leonard," she starts. "We can't be together the way we are. Abijah is my father in the sense that he made me like this."

"I was the only one in our clan who hadn't turned anyone, so, I figured, '*why not turn that little strumpet in town, the breadmaker's daughter?*' Little did I know, she can't even bake bread. Totally useless in the kitchen, man," Abijah says.

"Strumpet?"

"He's calling me a whore, basically," she says, looking away.

"Oh," I say. "So like, am I not the first human to fall for you?"

"Well, no, but you're the first human I've felt the same feelings for," she says.

"That's actually true, pal," Abijah says.

"So, we can't be together? Why tell me all this? Why have me meet you here? Did you guys dig the cave out?"

Abijah nods. "That was me."

"We can't be together with you being how you are. Being human. But, if you let me --"

"Turn me? That's the vampire part, I guess?"

She nods.

"So like, is he your ex?"

"Ugh, gross, man no, she's not my style," Abijah says. "Especially when she started with all that 'dad' stuff back in the 1800s."

"How old *are* you?" I ask her.

"I told you I was older than I looked. Abijah turned me back in 1896, so, I'm older than some things, but not others."

I think about her offer. To be like them. "Would I be able to see my friends and family ever again?"

"You'd never age. They would. Also, it's possible that you'd be risking our lives if you told them the truth about what you've become," she says.

"That's what happened to most of our kind," Abijah adds. "Humans started looking for us, and sure as shit, they found us."

"Can I think about it?"

Ebba sighs. She looks at Abijah. He shrugs. "By tonight?"

I nod.

"I'll be by around midnight, okay?"

I kiss her cheek and head toward the exit of the mine.

***

I spend most of the day thinking about her offer. The implications of living forever are different than that of immortality, I suppose. If man destroyed "most of their kind," as Abijah put it, then I'd still be able to die, I just wouldn't age or die naturally. Judging by Ebba, physical strength clearly goes up, plus the ability to fly is pretty cool, too. Who doesn't want to fly?

But not being able to tell my family and friends. Drinking occasional blood. Where does one source blood anyway? Would I have to kill people? Buy it? She didn't say she drank it all the time, but still. These are pretty powerful reasons one wouldn't want to engage in a lifestyle of living forever.

I play fetch with the dogs. I call my mom. I think more about Ebba's offer and the lifestyle we'd be leading. What if I get tired of her? Or she gets tired of me? How do I keep her interested *forever*? Is it for forever?

***

That night, when Ebba shows up, I'm nervously pacing around the foyer of the house. The dogs are asleep deeper into the house, and when she comes in, I kiss her and she wraps her arms around me.

"I know this hasn't been easy to think about all day. I wish I was given the option instead of Abijah just forcing it on me," she says.

"I'm still foggy on your relationship with him, other than calling him your 'dad' or whatever. Have you two slept together?"

She nods. "We were together for a time. About a hundred years or so."

"A hundred years? Fuck, that's longer than all my friends' relationships combined."

She laughs. "I couldn't deal with it anymore. What he did. I pushed it out of my mind for decades, but it always came back, like, he *forced* me to become this, I didn't ask him to turn me. I didn't ask for anything."

We sit on the porch and drink some wine.

"So, how do we get the blood that we drink?"

"The blood-drinking isn't that big a deal, you don't have to. Like, if you order a steak super rare, that'll take care of it. It's like a craving, every atom in your body cries out for it, but like I said, a steak, very rare, and you'll be fine," she says.

"Did you drink my blood?"

She gestures at my neck. "I couldn't resist, I had to taste you."

"That's both the hottest and weirdest thing I've ever heard," I say, smiling.

"I would completely understand if you didn't want to go through with this, Leonard. As I said, if I was given the option, I probably wouldn't go for it, either."

"Do you mean that?"

"I watched my entire family pass away. Saw my parents struggle when I was taken by Abijah and turned. They lived many more years, but in the end, I couldn't even attend their funerals. It wasn't easy. It still isn't. They're buried in the old cemetery in Resting Hollow. I visit them sometimes," she says, her voice cracking a bit. She steadies herself. "But, I've seen wonders. I've seen the birth of modern technology. I've seen buildings rise and fall. I've seen great leaders and historical monsters come to power. Witnessing the passage of history is incredible. Impactful moments experienced in real time, with the wisdom to understand the impact is a precious thing."

"That sounds amazing," I say, staring at her. "Show me your true self again. I want to see you."

She smiles. That same glow of blue-white light. I still shield my eyes, and when the light dims, she's sitting next to me, looking as she did in the cave, in all her vampire-fairy glory.

"So your kind doesn't have a name? That's where the vampire and fairy mythos comes from, so, like, do the vampire weaknesses apply?"

"Obviously not, I can walk in the sun. I love garlic. A stake through the heart would kill anyone, wouldn't it? Silver? I love silver, it's beautiful."

"Isn't silver for werewolves?"

She shrugs. "The point is, we aren't monsters. We're just people with a sad gift."

I lean in and kiss her. "I like you like this. I like you every way, I think."

"You still think I'm pretty like this?"

I nod. "Very much so."

We make love on the couch. After, she's tracing her finger on my chest and telling me about her life. About history. About the things she's seen.

"This place, the Palisades, as your people call it, I'm tied to it. I can leave, but not for very long. I must always return to the mountains, and now that it's been found, the spring. Something to do with our powers. Abijah never told me, most likely because he doesn't know."

"If I do this. If you turn me, I want to be able to see my family and friends. I'm not going to disappear from their lives," I say. "I guess it's like having my cake and eating it, too, but I refuse to give up my life entirely. I love you, but I love them, too."

"You love me?"

She looks at me. I kiss her and tell her I do. She tells me the same.

"Are you sure you want to be turned? There's no going back."

I shrug. "If I get tired of you, you can stake me in the heart. Fair?"

She smiles. We kiss for a long time, and her lips find their way to my neck. It's not like the movies. The small cut on my neck opens easily and she licks away the tiny bit of blood that trickles out.

She extends her right wrist and with a flick of her left pointer finger, she cuts herself with a fingernail. "Drink," she tells me.

I put my mouth on her wrist. I swallow a bit of her blood. The coppery taste fills my mouth, and shakes me to the core. It's like having a bloody nose, but somehow worse, because the blood isn't your own. I notice the cut on her wrist heal in a matter of seconds, and she returns to kissing my neck.

Maybe because I've seen too many movies, I expect the process to be like in *The Lost Boys* or something, and I prepare myself for a sudden flood of intense pain or pleasure or the wisdom of the centuries to suddenly be imparted to me. That never happens. We end up enjoying each other's bodies on the couch for a while, then head up to the bedroom.

***

The next morning, we wake up together. She's sleeping and looks perfect, so I carefully slip out of bed and head to the bathroom. Catching my reflection in the mirror, I notice my features have changed a bit. My ears have grown the same knife-like edge at the top of the ridge. My fangs have come in. My eyes look larger, somehow, too.

"Controlling your looks is the easiest power to master," she says, sounding tired.

"How?"

"Concentrate on what you looked like before. Think about your face. Your teeth. All of it."

I do as she says. In the mirror, the light blinds me, and instinctively, I rub them, hard. When I reopen my eyes, I'm back to normal. "It's ridiculous that it's so easy to do that."

I relieve myself then head back to bed. I snuggle in close to her and kiss her back. She smiles and moans and grabs my face, kissing me. "What do you want to do today?"

"Just this, if possible," I say, smiling.

"Won't your friends be home today?"

"Tonight, yeah," I can't stop kissing her. She tastes and smells so good, it's impossible to resist.

"So, then let's enjoy each other today, and tonight, we'll explore the mountains and forest together," she says. "I'll show you how to see in the dark."

We spend the day swimming, playing with the dogs, and making love all over the house. I decide not to tell my friends that last part when they get home around six that night. I introduce them to Ebba, and they seem to recognize her from around the area but can't put their finger on it.

"I'm always around, so, I'm sure we've bumped into each other before," she says.

"She's a cutie, man, good for you, how old is she?" Davis whispers as Ebba and I are leaving.

***

In the forest, I notice how black the leaves look at night, almost as if I'm seeing them for the first time. Ebba is standing behind me and coaching me on how to see in the dark. This isn't anywhere near as easy as changing how I look. After about an hour, I focus on a cluster of trees and the night seems to fade away.

The trunks of the trees, the greenery, even animals that I never knew were there suddenly have a purple-gray outline to them. "I think I'm doing it," I tell Ebba. I watch as the wind blows through the trees, focused intently on the treetops swaying in the darkness. Around us, I hear the rustling of leaves, of the wind howling, of bats and birds fluttering around the sky.

"Can you hear it? The vision and the sound often go hand in hand, especially early on," she whispers, almost inaudibly.

"I can."

After watching the night for a while, I close my eyes and she takes my hand and leads me into the mountains. She shows me the town from a vantage point close to the top, which is easy to climb when you can fly up certain sections. Flying is surprisingly easy, even though what I'm doing is like jumping very high and kinda' far.

"All the movies that say it takes a long time to 'hone your powers' or whatever are bullshit," she tells me. "It's all special effects, anyway. If they just protected the rights of our people and made us citizens, we could make a ton of money for the movies with the stuff we can do."

The palisades is beautiful from up here. Further away, I see Resting Hollow, too. The lights from the town are scattered and perfect.

"I wish we could stay up here. To live, I mean," I say.

"Why couldn't we?"

She rests her head on my shoulder. I kiss her forehead. "You still haven't told me where you live. Where do you sleep?"

She points into the woods. "Abijah built a small cabin in the woods."

"I don't suppose there's room for the three of us, huh?"

She shakes her head. "I'm sorry, I didn't think about that."

"It's okay, we'll make it work. Maybe it's time you moved out of your 'dad's' house?"

She laughs. "I guess so."

"How about tonight, we fly back to my place in Resting Hollow, go to bed and figure out the next steps then?"

"That sounds perfect. I should get some of my things from Abijah first, though."

We kiss and do our fly/jump thing down the side of the mountain, and through the woods, the branches of trees whipping our faces as we leap through the canopy above.

***

Ebba and I spend the next half a year or so going to different places all over the east coast. She says our powers won't let us leave the continental United States for some reason (something to do with our powers being tied to the soil on which we were turned), so we return to Resting Hollow and the Palisades after every trip. I fall even more in love with her every day, and she's just brilliant, funny and a pleasure to have around.

We use our powers to get whatever we need, which is stealing, sure, but at a certain point, things are only material, so, we've, in a way, evolved past the notion of stealing. It's a very bohemian way of looking at things, but that's Ebba. She's a free spirit and she's rubbed off on me a lot. Using our powers is a gift and the world has taken so much from so many, so taking some back isn't a bad deal.

We watch the sun rise from atop the Empire State Building. We eat sushi while floating above Niagara Falls. We talk to spirits at Gettysburg. Touristy shit. Using our powers not at all for good, but for ourselves.

Periodic trips to the spring in the mountain turn into ritualistic experiences for us upon return. Sometimes we bathe in the spring, sometimes we make love in it. The icy bite of the water doesn't have much of an impact on us anymore.

On one of the return trips, Ebba mentions that we should go see Abijah, that there's unfinished business with him. Not knowing what she could possibly have to say to him, I go along anyway, half hoping that he's not at home.

Abijah's cabin is small, but well maintained. He's inside, reading, he looks tired, run down. "Wait here," Ebba tells me.

She goes inside and I hear the two of them talking. I listen closely but can't make out everything they're saying. Suddenly, the crash of what sounds like glass startles me and I rush into the cabin to see Abijah standing over Ebba, who's holding her forehead, a mirror behind her, on the wall, smashed to pieces.

"This wasn't the plan, Ebba!"

In a second, Abijah's on her. She struggles in his grasp, and I rush to her, but Abijah tosses me aside without much difficulty. He's choking her, and her eyes are wide. She starts to glow, revealing her true self, but he does, too. Only when the light fades, he doesn't look much like he did before.

His fangs are longer. Sharper than Ebba's or my own. His skin has taken on a shade of maroon unlike anything I've ever seen in reality. His head somehow looks bigger. He has two bony protrusions above his ears.

The thing that scares me the most is the tail. It whips around wildly, uncontrolled, throwing itself all over the place, like it has a mind of its own. Terrified, I charge him again, jumping on his back. While he's distracted, Ebba slashes his throat with her nails. The cut is deep and blood spurts everywhere.

He tosses me across the room through his kitchen table. Grabbing one of the splintered legs, I charge him again and drive the piece of wood directly into where I hope his heart is. Abijah roars and collapses at my feet. He whimpers a bit as the life drains from his neck and the stake in his chest.

Ebba walks over to me and takes my hand. "Are you okay?"

I nod. "Are you?"

She nods, staring at Abijah's body on the floor.

"What did he mean when he said that thing about 'the plan?'" I ask.

She sighs. "He was crazy. He talked about how easy it would be to take back Resting Hollow from the world of men. He said that my connection to you was the key."

I look at her. "The key? How? I'm just a painfully normal guy."

"Like I said, he was crazy. He thought you'd turn more people and over time, we'd have the whole town."

We walk out of the cabin. "Did you only turn me because he wanted you to? Was this all a plan?"

She sighs. "In the beginning, yes, it was all bullshit, but I got to actually know you, and well, I feel the way I feel. I used my powers in the beginning, yes, but after the first couple of times I saw you, I didn't need to."

"Powers? What do you mean?"

"Some people, throughout the centuries, have referred to what I am as a, well …" she trails off. "As a succubus. Do you know what that is?"

"Sort've. Am I a succubus, too?"

"No, you'd be an incubus, I guess, that's the male version. Basically, part of our powers is that we can seduce people and use their sex drives against them, if we want to. I did that to you, and I'm sorry."

I can't even look at her in this moment. Something just doesn't feel right inside me. In my chest. I'm not upset that she lied to me. People lie, that's what we do, but the fact that she made me change who I am. That's the part that hurts the most. I've become something that's just human enough to live, but not human enough to make longlasting connections with anyone. She's changed me. To the core.

She goes to put her hand on my shoulder, but I brush her away. "Don't touch me right now."

She recoils. "Leonard, please, the past few months, everything's been so perfect with you. Please, don't pull away from me."

"What the fuck was he, Ebba? He didn't look like us."

"Abijah was closer to the veil than you and me. He almost died when he turned, and when he made the change, he was different. Something came back with him, that's why he looked different," she tells me, her eyes tearing up.

"You lied to me, about a lot," I start. She tries to touch me again, but I pull away.

"The past six months weren't a lie, Leonard, I swear," she pleads.

"How can I trust you? You turned me into this monster and I didn't even question it because I was crazy about you, and my life just wasn't what I was hoping it could've been. Then you come along and offer me this horrible gift, and I just go along with it?"

I look at the broken mirror. Ebba's blood on the shards. Her wound has healed during our conversation.

"I'm going to see my family," I finally say, before leaving the cabin and flying off into the night.

***

That night, I softly land on the back porch of my parents' house. I knock on the door and my old man is sitting, watching the Yankees beat the Royals. He opens the door and asks where I've been.

"Sorry I haven't been around too much. Traveling a lot, finding myself, that kinda' thing," I say.

"Well, we love when you call, but it'd be nice to see your face more, kiddo," he says.

I sit down. Dad hands me a beer. "Where's mom?"

"At one of her knitting meetings, she goes like four nights a week now."

"That's cool."

We watch the baseball game for a while. I don't even know how to start the conversation with him. We have another beer and sit in silence for a long while. Eventually, he dozes off and I'm sitting there, alone.

Standing up, I walk over to him, kiss him on the forehead, open the sliding door and fly off into the night.

***

I fly for a long time. I find myself floating above Times Square. Below me, even at this late hour, people bustle about the neon corridors of the city, bathed in electric glow. No one seems to notice me up here. In all the places Ebba and I went to, no one suspected anything. No one knew what we were. No one cared that we were flying above them. No one noticed.

These people below, with their phones and devices, if they only looked up, would see me in a heartbeat. This isn't a movie, I'm not a vampire wearing all black to blend in. I'm very easily seen if people would just look. But I guess that's the blessing of who we are. The blessing of immortality and power, knowing that we can vanish if we need to, because of what we are and the hesitance of people to believe in that.

All it took for me to believe in it was a cute girl in a white dress.

The problem is whether or not I can trust that girl in the white dress.

***

I find Ebba at the spring the next morning. She's got her feet in the water and is staring into the cool water. Her face is puffy, red, like she's been crying. She looks up at me. She's still crying, actually.

"I'm not sure what to say, Ebba. You really fucked this up," I say.

She nods. "I'm sorry I misled you in the beginning. If I could take it back, I would, I'm just -- I'm sorry."

"I really love you, you know? Not like how I've ever loved anyone before. It's different for me now, things just feel different, like, love feels different, maybe because now I know we have eternity, I just don't know," I say, rambling a bit.

She nods. "We do have eternity. I'll spend every day of that eternity trying to make things up to you."

I stare at her. I can tell she's being sincere. "Do our powers work on each other?"

"What?"

"Do our powers, like the ones you manipulated me with in the beginning, do they still work on each other once we've turned?"

She looks at the water. "No. If they did, wouldn't I just use them to make you love me again?"

"That's the thing, I do love you. I should be filled with anger, but I'm not. I'm worried you're whammying me again, Ebba."

"I'm not, I swear," she says, angry.

"That's the thing, I don't know. How can I ever trust you?"

She sighs. "I understand. Leonard, you were an amazing partner in life and in what we are. Something in-between, I suppose. You never failed to tell me how pretty I looked, to tell me you loved me. You were perfect and I love you for it."

I walk over to her and put my arms around her. She smells amazing, like always. "You're the prettiest thing I've ever seen in my entire life."

She smiles. "Your entire life is forever, now."

She stands up and starts down the darkened mine, following the spring. "Maybe I'll see you around sometime."

"Maybe," I say, watching her walk slowly and delicately down the mine.

I remain at the spring for a little while longer, until she's totally out of sight. Eventually, I exit the mine and stare at the night sky. Rising slowly, I feel the wind whip around me as I head ever-skyward.

The Veil

The space left behind after a person dies is perhaps the worst part. The loss of a parent, no matter how old they were, or how sudden or whatever the case may be, leaves a void that can't be filled. These are the things I talk about in my group counseling sessions. Every week, I feel like I'm treading the same water, talking about the same things, and knowing that everyone's probably bored hearing me talk about this. *Just get over it, already. Be a man. He's gone. Let it go.*

Nobody says these things, but how could they not be thinking it?

When I leave the session, I walk quickly to my car, get in, and music blasts from the speakers. I start to cry thinking about my dad. His last days on this planet, bleeding from his arms because his skin was so thin and his blood pooling in his hospital bed. How when I'd visit him, he never looked comfortable, and always had his feet dangling off the bed, wearing those stupid no-slip socks they give patients. How confused and generally out of it he looked. How his voice, once booming and powerful, had escaped him in the months since getting sick.

I drive back to my apartment and get a text from my sister, asking how the counseling session went. I lie and tell her it was great. There's no point in letting her into my mind, how I'm not recovering. How I'm getting worse. I think about visiting the grave, but I know that dad's around me all the time. We used to watch a lot of *Seinfeld* and I remember one where Jerry's aunt or grandmother or somebody dies and he jokes about how they're out in the galaxy now, why would they waste their time hanging around the people they knew in life?

But knowing my dad, he'd hang around. I just wish I could talk to him one last time. Our final conversation was about how I was going to visit him the next morning, because I was busy heading into the city to see Interpol perform at Madison Square Garden. When I got home around one in the morning, I went to bed, and about an hour later, dad was taking his final breaths.

I walk into a small office in my apartment and look at all the strange technology and machinery that I've bought over the last couple months since dad died. Electromagnetic field detectors. Infrared cameras. I bought an old XBOX Kinect off eBay and hooked it up to my computer, so I can get a constant loop of the room around me, everything cast in gray, hoping to pick up something. The latest toy I picked up is a "spirit box," a thing that cycles through radio frequencies and singles out certain words, the theory behind it being that something is trying to communicate.

I guess I've become an amateur ghost hunter since dad died. None of this stuff has worked so far. None of it has connected me to him. None of it has yielded results in any way at all and I feel a tinge of regret and sadness every time I try to use one of them. The spirit box may even be broken, since the damn thing just makes static all the time, whenever I turn it on.

I check the Kinect camera. Nothing. I pour some whiskey and sit down, watching the video loop of the office. Nothing is moving. Not even myself. I look ghostly white, my eyes washed out black in the view from the camera. The only movement is the occasional sip of whiskey.

Turning on the television, I set up an old video camera and point it directly at the screen, creating what paranormal researchers call a "feedback loop." Once the camera is fired up, I stare at the small viewfinder screen on the side, at the television, and wait. I pull up a small stool I have, grab my whiskey, and watch for over an hour for something to appear in the viewfinder. Nothing ever does. Just the static of the television. I didn't even know how to get static on a 42" plasma screen, but here we are, a quick Google search, and boom, it works.

After the feedback loop fails to produce any results, I sit down in my favorite chair and start to watch a movie, with feigned interest. I text my mother to see how she's doing, and she doesn't respond. A friend texts to check in on me, and we talk for a little while about how I'm feeling. I'm glad to have friends who are so understanding and helpful in some moments. Other times, nothing helps. Times like when I'm lying in bed, praying that dad will contact me somehow. Times when I fixate on our last conversation. Times when I think about enjoying my favorite band at the greatest venue in the world and knowing my father's time on this planet was running out.

At work, I find my thoughts drifting more and more frequently. The work I do is mindless, so, it doesn't matter much. Nothing really does, I suppose, but I keep playing our final conversation over and over in my head. I think about how the last time I saw him, I failed to kiss him goodbye, thinking that there was so much dried blood all over his arm and shoulder, and that I couldn't handle that. This was two days before he died.

I walk over to my record collection and put on one of dad's favorites - The Four Seasons.

At work is when my darkest thoughts come to me. Managing a hardware store isn't tough work, and I'm surrounded by tools that would give me the fast track to see my dad again. I think about how I'd do it all the time.

Hammer to the face? *Too bloody.*

Chainsaw to the wrists? *How would I hold it?*

Saw blade to my arteries? *See "hammer to the face?"*

In the end, I always come to the conclusion that the items at my store would result in someone else having to clean up the mess. Even the rat and bug poisons we stock would make me vomit all over the place before I shuffled off this mortal coil. I wish I could get a gun. I thought about texting a buddy of mine who's a cop and asking him for a gun, but I chickened out.

Deep down, I don't want to die, but knowing that my dad is gone, I just can't bear the thought of living. Selfish, I know. What would my mother do? My sister? My niece and nephew?

They'd be fine, I find myself thinking while holding a box cutter in my hand at work.

"Hello?"

I look up and see a young woman across from me, on the other side of the counter. My hand, knuckles white, still grip the box cutter.

"Sorry, dazed out there a second," I say, ringing the box cutter up. I notice she's wearing a Strokes t-shirt, and I make a mental note to listen to their records later.

"No worries. Thanks!" she says, giving me a strange little side-smile, and leaving the store.

That night, I settle into the same routine. The feedback loop. The Kinect camera. The EMF detector. The spirit box. Same results. I put on The Strokes' "Is This It" and recline in my favorite chair.

The next day, at work, my mom returns my text and tells me she has to go out of town to take care of some business with my aunt knowing that this is code for "go to Atlantic City and spend the money your father left me."

"Sounds good, if you need anything, let me know."

"Why don't you take a trip or something, sweetie? You've been so down lately," mom says.

"Where would I go?"

After a long pause, she says "Somewhere. Anywhere."

I nod, tell her I love her and that I'll check in on the house while she's gone.

Two weeks or so later, I'm back at the counseling group, keeping quiet, making myself a cup of coffee and eating a donut that's dropping powdered sugar all over my shirt when she walks in. Strokes girl. She walks in, sheepishly, and takes a seat. I notice something sticking out of the sleeves of her hoodie.

I brush the powdered sugar off my shirt and walk over to the circle of regulars ready to share and steal the occasional glimpse at Strokes girl. She looks anxious. Ready to sprint to the door at a moment's notice. I keep looking at her sleeves trying to see what's sticking out, but I can't quite make it out.

Eventually, the coordinator for the meeting looks around the room and says "Anyone else care to share?" The coordinator's eyes land on me, but I'm glancing at Strokes girl.

"I'll go," Strokes girl volunteers. I nearly jump when she breaks the silence.

"About a month or so ago, my grandma died, and I've been having a hard time ever since." She rolls up the sleeves of her hoodie, revealing that she's got bandages up and down her wrist. "I tried to take myself out of the game, to see her again, to have one more talk with her, but, I didn't make it, I came back, and I don't know if I'll try again, but I was so close."

Boxcutter girl, not Strokes girl.

"Do I need to tell you my name or anything," she asks. The coordinator tells her that she doesn't have to. I'm dying to know her name.

"Anyway, that's my story," she says, rolling her sleeves back down.

The coordinator tells her some basic grief counseling nonsense that doesn't really work, and we wrap our meeting. It is the first time since I've started coming to these that I haven't spoken about my dad. Strokes girl (Boxcutter girl?) gets up and heads for the exit, and I do, too.

Outside, she's struggling to light a cigarette, since her lighter doesn't seem to be working. I just stand there, watching her. "Hey," I eventually say.

She looks up, finishes lighting her cigarette. "You look familiar."

"Umm, well, I'm the manager of the hardware store. You came in and bought a box cutter couple'a weeks back," I say, stammering a bit.

"Oh shit, that's right," she says. She offers me a cigarette.

"I'm good, thanks," I say, walking closer. "So, I'm sorry that happened."

She stares at me. "Sorry about what?"

"Your grandmother. I can relate. My dad died a little while ago, that's why I'm here."

"Oh. I'm sorry, too. Does it get easier?"

I shake my head. "Not for me, it hasn't. Wish I could say it does."

"Figures," she says, taking a long drag off the cigarette.

"Everyone always looks so cool when they smoke. Should I start smoking?"

"Do I look cool when I smoke? With the mummy bandages and everything?" We share a laugh.

"As cool as a mummy can, I suppose," I say.

We exchange numbers. A few days later, she texts me to talk about her grandmother. She asks about my dad. We talk about everything. She's a couple years younger than me, moved here five years ago from the city, looking to work on her doctorate in music at the local university. Decided to stay and teach at the same place after they offered her a job. She doesn't live in town; instead, she lives in an old converted farmhouse on the highway outside of town. We compare notes on local restaurants, bars, movies, the usual stuff.

When the conversation turns to music, she's impressed with my knowledge and practically begs to see my records. I half apologetically tell her that I have over a thousand "pieces of vinyl," as I refer to them. She laughs at that. She laughs a lot. At me. At life in general.

The following week, at the counseling meeting, she and I sit across from each other and listen to others. We don't talk. Instead, we go to a diner after the meeting and talk more. We reflect on what the others in the meeting said, and talk about therapeutic ideas we read about online or heard from others in the group, or came up with on our own. I discuss the benefits of drinking heavily, a sentiment she shares.

After the diner, she hands me a cigarette and tells me to be "one of the cool kids," so I light it up and start puffing. I don't cough, oddly enough, like so many do in movies and TV shows when they smoke their first cigarette. Instead, I find it relaxing.

"Wow," she says, staring at me.

"What?"

"I've never seen anyone look so cool in my entire life," she says, trying not to crack up laughing.

We head back to her place, and when I walk in, I see candles, religious items, camera equipment and other stuff that looks all too familiar. She pauses and suddenly realizes that all of her stuff is scattered around the living room. A video camera is pointing at the television creating an endless feedback loop.

"Umm, so, yeah, this probably looks a little psycho, right?" She asks, sounding genuinely nervous.

"Only a little," I say. "You don't have a spirit box, though."

"How do you --" She pauses. After a moment, she leans in and kisses me. I kiss her back.

I take her to breakfast the next morning, with intentions of asking her about how she learned about the equipment and the ghost hunting stuff, but she launches right into it. "I don't know if I believe in the spirit box thing. Like, it seems so phony, I dunno," she says, stuffing scrambled eggs in her mouth.

"It's never worked right for me, so I can understand that," I admit.

"I've been thinking about what to do in terms of my next steps," she tells me.

"What do you mean?"

"Like, using a witch board or some other form of contact."

"A witch board? Like, a Ouija board?"

She nods. I sit back and think about it. "They always say in all those ghost shows and movies and stuff not to fuck with a Ouija board. Supposedly invites bad stuff in. This is that moment in the horror movie where they lay out that using one of those boards is a bad idea," I say, half laughing, trying to hide my genuine nervousness.

She smiles. "Then this also must be the part of the horror movie where the intrepid ghost hunters ignore the warnings and goes ahead with their clearly terrible plan?"

I nod.

"Will you do it with me?" she asks.

I think for a minute. "Sure."

A few days go by before Amazon delivers my brand-new Ouija board. That night, I head to her house, we light some candles, set the board up, drink some wine, put on a "spooky sounds" playlist on Spotify and sit across from each other, the board between us.

She's wearing her Strokes t-shirt again and I think back to the first time I met her, when I sold her the box cutter she used to try to kill herself. *The world is a strange place*, I think to myself when she gives me a little side-mouth smile that sends chills up my spine.

We follow the directions packed in the Ouija board box, using the planchette and asking simple yes and no questions. The planchette never moves. I don't even jokingly nudge it. Neither does she.

After trying for the better part of an hour, she looks frustrated. Standing quickly, she storms away from the board. I rise and follow her. She walks out the back door onto the porch, which is lit with paper lanterns, and lights a cigarette.

"I'm sorry, we should keep trying," I say.

She shakes her head. "This is all such bullshit. She's not out there. She's nowhere," she says, tears welling up. I wrap my arms around her, but she pushes me away, "Not now, I don't want that."

I back away. Her arms are bare, with the stitches visible. They look like dark roots running down the length of her arms from the bicep to the wrist. I never paid attention to how high up on her arm she started tearing herself open. I imagine the blood she must have lost. She never told me about the blood. She told me about where she did it, in her bathtub, which has since been replaced, because the stains of blood on the white tub couldn't be totally removed. There must have been a lot.

"I'm sorry. I know you're just trying to comfort me. I really love that about you," she says, finally, after a long silence between us.

"I care a lot about you, I'm sorry it didn't work," I say again. "We can keep trying. One time doesn't mean it doesn't work."

She looks at me. Her face is red and swollen from crying. "You're right."

"I rarely am, but I think in this case, I might be," I say. She laughs. That side-smile returns. She kisses me.

"We can keep trying," she says, wrapping her arms around me. "However long it takes, right?"

I nod. "Yep."

She kisses me and takes my hand and we dance on the porch, moving slowly and rhythmically in the night, back and forth, to the tune of chains rattling and cauldrons bubbling on the playlist.

Out of the corner of my eye, I see the planchette move.

Bear Hands

"Resting Hollow Man Mauled to Death by Bear - Remains Partially Eaten"

That's what the headline of the Resting Hollow Tribune read the day after they found your devoured and demolished body not far from your truck off the main highway into town. You were a local shop teacher in the middle school, teaching kids about woodworking, making CO_2 cars and clocks they can take home to their parents at the end of the semester.

You were my best friend. We grew up together, our moms having been co-workers at the federal building outside town. You liked to say we went through all those awkward phases together. Puberty. Girls. We'd share stories of our clumsy fumblings in the back of darkened movie theaters and the back of my older brother's car at the local drive-in.

When you got the job to teach shop class, we grabbed a beer at Talbot's Pub, one of the better bars in town. When I opened my garage and became a mechanic, we hit Talbot's again. When you got married, I was your best man. Your wife, Jenny, she's a good girl. Helluva good cook. Smart as a whip.

Your son is my godson. It's my job to make sure your boy is raised right in the eyes of the Lord. That your boy grows up with God in his heart. That he grows up to be a good, righteous man.

I never thought that I'd have to step up to the plate in that department. The day we put what was left of you into your family's plot, I looked your boy in the eye and told him that I loved him very much. And that I was going to make sure we honor and remember his daddy. That we always keep you in our hearts and minds.

And then I leaned closer and told your son that I was going to hunt and kill the bear that killed my best friend. With my bare hands if I had to.

That night, I started building things in my shed. I had brought home spare parts from my garage, a few car batteries. Some coils. Springs. Metal rods. I wasn't sure what I was building, but as I played with the pieces, things began to take shape.

I thought about you. My best friend. My closest confidant. You knew all my secrets. Knew about the time I had stolen the captain of the baseball team's best girl for a night of dancing and more at a fancy bar outside of town. Knew about the time I soaped the police chief's windows after he told my old man that he saw me sneaking into the movie theater with my old gal.

As my mind thought back to all the good times we had, I had made something. Using the rod, I had fastened two jagged pieces of a car door to the end, making a crude spear. The coil ran down to the midpoint of the rod, creating a kind of metal slide like the kind you see at the local pool. It was like that "highway hypnosis" you read about. I just kinda' worked, absentminded, for hours, until this *thing* was ready.

Getting stuck with the business end of this spear would certainly not be a pleasurable experience.

I put on some of our favorite tunes. Some of that music the kids today consider "classic rock." I lit a cigarette and started using a blowtorch to add pieces of jagged metal to a pair of brass knuckles my old man gave me from his time fighting the Nazis.

By the time I was done with the brass knuckles, they looked positively medieval. It had also become morning. Early morning. Dusk. The sky was burning orange-purple. You had been in the ground less than sixteen hours.

I took a break and went into the house, sweaty and a little exhausted. I grabbed the glass bottle of milk in the fridge and downed what was left of it, then sat at the kitchen table. My best friend was with me when I bought this place a few years ago. We had worked on putting in the wood floors in the living room a few months ago.

We watched the last two Super Bowls in there, too.

I grabbed a bag of beef jerky from the cupboard. A couple cans of pop and a few beers from the fridge. I went upstairs and grabbed my old backpack; I loaded the jerky, beer and pop into the bag. I grabbed a small canteen and filled it with water. I took a swig.

I placed the bag in the front seat of my truck, next to the spear and the brass knucks. I then went back upstairs to shave, use the bathroom, and shower. Once back in my bedroom, I lit a cigarette while dressing. I sat at the edge of my bed and rested my bones a minute before getting dressed and putting on cologne. You used to make fun of me for sticking with Old Spice, but it's what I've always used.

When I got back downstairs, Jenny was sitting on the couch. She was staring at me, waiting. She must've let herself in with the key I gave you when I bought the house.

"What're you doin'?" Her eyes are red and puffy, I assume from crying.

"Nothin'. Everything okay?"

"The kid told me what you said yesterday. About going into the woods."

I stare at her. Shuffle a bit, uneasy.

"You know I can't let you do that, right?"

Not looking at her, staring at an empty spot on the ceiling, I tell her "I got to."

She stands up and walks over to the fireplace. On the mantle that picture of you and her on your wedding day catches her eye, the one where you're surrounded by the wedding party. She stares at it.

"Please don't. I can't lose you, too," she says.

"Ya' ain't losin' me, Jenny. Nobody else dies. It's just somethin' I gotta' do. You ain't a man, you don't understand."

Rolling her eyes, she started crying. "I ain't a man, because I don't get stupid ideas like this in my head."

Smiling, I know she's right.

I walk over to her and put my hand on her shoulder. "I'll be back before the weekend. I promise."

That gives me three days to track and kill the bear that killed you. All I know is what the medical report said. Large bear. Black (based on hairs found on your remains). Large mouth. Apparently responsible for a reduction in the deer population over the last few years judging by local scuttlebutt. Also supposedly has a hairless spot and scar on its belly from getting clipped by a hunter four years back.

"What if you don't come back?"

I look around the room. Clear my throat. Put on my lucky New York Yankees hat. "Take the house. Sell my stuff. Sell everything. Start a college fund for the kid." Jenny wraps her arms around me softly. She smells like the cool air and vanilla. She kisses me on the cheek and leaves.

I glance at the picture of all of us on your wedding day. I light another cigarette, get into my truck, and drive off to where your truck was found on the side of the highway.

Once there, I get out of the car, walk to the tree line, light a cigarette and walk in. Slung over my shoulder is the spear. Tucked in my jacket pocket are the brass knuckles. I have a survival knife at my hip that I got as a Christmas present when I was a kid from my uncle, who was a bit of an outdoorsman. It has a compass on the hilt, which I'm hoping helps track down the location of where your body was found.

I'm not sure why you were in the woods. No one is, really. The idea was that maybe you stopped to take a piss and got pulled into the woods by the bear. This made some sense, I guess, but then again, who knows? Did bears pull people into the woods like that? Would a bear pull you along for almost a mile before leaving your remains where they were?

I push the thought of your final moments out of my head and continue on into the woods. I eventually arrive at a clearing, sit on a downed tree and take a swig of water. I have a small tent in my backpack that I've had since I was a kid (another gift from my woodsman uncle), along with a sleeping bag rolled up and slung over my shoulder. I'm ready to spend a few nights here if I have to. Whatever it takes. I have to kill that bear.

I continue on, finding the spot where you were discovered. The area has markers on it from the park rangers who found you, each with a number on them.

I think of you being found here. How mangled your body was. How the strength of this bear would've been too much for you. For anyone. I wonder if you were dead by the time you made it here or if the bear was a sadist and carried you along, thrashing your body around and then tearing your throat out right here, delivering the final blow.

I remember when you and I were kids and your old cat, Jingles, caught a mouse. It didn't kill it right away. Instead it batted it around, chased it, cornered it, then when it got bored, Jingles sunk its teeth into the mouse and tore its head off. You threw up when you saw that happen but I stared, mesmerized by the brutality of it.

I eat some jerky. Drink a beer. Light a cigarette. I regret not buying another pack before I got out here because I only have three cigarettes left. Before I know it, it's night.

I set up the tent, start a small fire, and sit in the dark listening to the woods around me. As the fire flickers, shadows dance all over, creating an almost rhythmic gyration of light and movement, my eyes playing tricks on me.

It isn't too cold, so my jeans and hoodie are enough, and I take my jacket, wrap it around the food bag I have, and hang it in a nearby tree, away from my tent. High enough that no small critter can get to it. But a large, angry, scarred black bear? Now that would be a different story.

The fire dies on its own and I slip into the tent. The spear is next to me. I keep my hand on it until I fall asleep, which doesn't happen quickly. It feels like I just shut my eyes when suddenly it's morning and I have to get back out there.

I grab the food pack, which is undisturbed, pack up the tent, sleeping bag and more, and venture further into the woods.

Bears make their beds under rocks, I remember reading when I was a kid. Sometimes they plop down in a big hole in the ground. Sometimes under a fallen tree. They aren't picky, I guess. I remember my uncle telling me that some black bears are even nocturnal. I didn't know what that meant at the time, but I know now that it means they like to hang out at night, looking for food.

I guess me and you were nocturnal, too. We liked late nights, drinking at Talbot's, drinking at the bluff, looking out on the town. Watching as the different houses' lights turned off one by one until the entire town was asleep. We started doing that when our folks let us ride our bikes wherever we wanted, as long as we were home for supper.

While walking, I notice there's a breeze that's picked up. The sky is gray. It looks like rain, but the air is crisp. I squeeze the spear tightly in my hand and continue onward. I arrive at a small cliff, looking out on the stream we used to drink at in high school. I don't expect to find these old places while trying to find the monster that killed you. I don't expect it none at all.

I sit down and think about lighting a cigarette but pause when I realize there aren't many left. I watch the water surge past a little while, thinking about the times we had here. Was that why you came out here? A walk down memory lane? I don't remember the water being so violent this far downstream, but it rages, loudly.

"Hell with it," I say, lighting one of my few remaining smokes.

When I look up from blocking the wind and lighting my cig, I see him.

Black fur. Six feet long. Maybe 700 or so pounds. The missing fur. The scar. The bear watches me. I rise slowly, clutching the spear tighter.

I watch as the monster eyes me. We're separated by the water. I couldn't get to it if I tried. I hope and pray it can cross the water, so at least it's weighed down by the heft of the water on its fur.

But it just stares and breathes. I do the same.

Eventually, it turns its back and walks into the woods, disappearing after some time. I feel panic in my chest, the tightening of the muscles in my legs. My breath slowing, then returning. I watch carefully, waiting for the monster to return. I don't know what to do for a moment, but I think about this thing killing you and I remember why I'm here.

By the time I start moving again, the cigarette is dangling from my lip, half burnt out. I climb down the small cliffside and look for a way to cross the river. I walk south along the water for about a mile until I finally spot a shallow section with a fallen tree that stretches the gap. Taking my time and making sure I've got a good grip on my belongings, I move slowly across the gap. The water goes up to my knees, and it's rushing pretty fast, but not enough to knock me down.

Once across, I walk north, essentially retracing my steps to the area where I spotted the monster. Along the way, I see some deer, I see some birds that I don't know what they are, and the sky brightens up some. The wind still whips through the trees, but thankfully it isn't cold. Once I get to the area where I saw the monster, I stop and take a sip of water.

I sit on a large rock and take a bite of jerky. I think back to when we were in junior high and read that book about the boys on the island - *Lord of the Flies*, which we called *Lord of the Fries* because we were dumb kids, but anyway, I think back to when we were reading it and how our younger selves would think it was cool that I'm basically living it now. Maybe not totally, because no one's dropping rocks on my head or nothin', but I'm out here, roughing it in the woods. It's not a normal part of the routine. I think our younger selves would get a kick outta' that.

Taking out a small map of the area, I note roughly where I am. I make a mark on the map to indicate where I saw the monster, and a rough spot to indicate where I camped the night before. I look at the map and note other landmarks on it - the bluff, the river, obviously. The nearby town, the highway. Where your car was found. Where you were found. I sit, thinking about you, me, our lives, how different they were, but how much in common we had.

Life escapes us quickly. Time passes so quickly, even though when we're going through it, it drags. I remember you telling me about Jenny when you met her. She was at the local college, and you had just started teaching. How excited you were to have met her and how excited you were to go on your next date. When I met her, I knew she was the one for you.

I remember how, over the years, after Jenny moved in, how we started drifting. How life started taking root in who we are. How time and commitments started placing a wedge between us. But we worked hard to overcome it and see each other and spend as much time as possible, but it wasn't the same, and we both knew that. We never talked about it much, but we both knew it was true.

The changing of time, the changing of our lives. Friendships get harder the older you get. I was never as smart as you, but I think about things. Our other friends are good people, but they ain't you. My best friend is dead. And now there's a hole in my life. In his son's life. In his wife's life.

And I can't let that stand.

I don't realize that I'm crying, but when the wind blows, I feel cold on my cheeks, and wipe the tears away. I grab a beer, tear it open, down it quickly. Only a couple of them left. And they've certainly gotten warm.

I set up my campsite by the water, placing my remaining beers in the water, connected by a small string I brought with me, so they won't float away and they get cold again. I work up the courage and follow what I remember to be the path of the monster into the woods.

It's starting to get dark, and I've been walking a while, with no sight of the monster. I decide to turn back and return to the river and my campsite. The darkening sky creates almost a haze in the woods while I trek back. Over my shoulder, I hear the crackling of leaves and twigs. Pausing, I turn slowly, my hands firmly wrapped around the spear. I don't see anything, but I hear a similar sound to my left, and when I turn, I see nothing.

"Come on, you sonofabitch … do it," I mutter, my hands shaking a little at the adrenaline coursing through my body.

I hear a grumble behind me, a low, gut-sound. When I turn, I see two eyes glowing in the darkness about ten feet away from me. The spear is sturdy. It doesn't rattle even though I pieced it together myself in a daze of sadness and anger.

The eyes never move. They never get closer. I stare back. The sky gets darker. Eventually, the eyes recede into the darkness and vanish completely. I remain standing, ready. After what feels like hours, I relax a bit, and head back to the camp.

Sitting on the same rock as earlier, I watch the fire. The beers are cold, so I have another, and I finish my cigarettes. I promised Jenny I'd only be away the weekend and I intend to keep that promise. I'll head back tomorrow evening. Retrace my steps and head back to town. Back to work. Back to life.

That gut-sound. I hear it on the edge of my camp. Being near the river, the sound of the water is loud, but that gut-sound is somehow louder. My eyes dart upward and I see it - the monster. The spear is next to the fire, but my brass knucks are in my pocket. I slip them on.

"Now, then?" I say, rising. I take a step toward the spear, and the monster, moving carefully, eyes locked on me, moves closer to the fire, too.

Once close enough, I kneel down and grip the spear. The monster continues closer. Once it's close enough, I ready the spear and grip it tightly. More of those gut-sounds. It's close enough that I can see its drool. I can see the scar. The teeth.

I am scared for the last time in my life.

The monster swipes at the spear, but I move quickly, its large paw missing wide. I step closer to the monster, and he backs away a bit, sizing me up.

The monster steps closer and I ready the spear between its eyes. I stab at him, but he shifts out of the way. I feel adrenaline, excitement, and tightness in my legs all at the same time, and my heart pounds loudly in my chest, coursing the blood and adrenaline to every part of my body.

He swipes again, and this time I slash its arm, causing the monster to howl in pain. I howl back, advancing forward with the spear, slashing and stabbing wherever I can. I connect a few times, but the monster seems unaffected. He swipes at me, then charges, but I put the fire between us and it steps back.

Suddenly, the monster charges *through* the fire, roaring at me while it moves. Sparks and fiery logs fly everywhere, and I charge forward, screaming. When the monster rises into the air on its back legs, I panic at the enormity, and ready the spear.

As he falls, I think of you. I think of you and this monster. Your last moments. My screaming becomes frenzied. There's blood flying everywhere. It's like one of those horror movies we used to watch. My blood. The monster's. The spear is snapped in two. The monster is snapping at me, slashing when it can. I begin punching with the brass knuckles.

I connect, over and over, plunging the sharp tips into the monster's face, neck and haunches. It bellows and roars, and I do, too.

Eventually, there is stillness. The night sky is filled with stars and I drift off.

The next morning, I stir. I look over at the monster, its massive frame lying next to what was my fire. The broken spear still dug into its gut. I look down at my hands, at the bruises, the broken skin, fur, and my brass knuckles, covered in monster blood.

I think about removing the spear from the monster's stomach, but push the thought out of my head. I walk to the water's edge and look for my last few beers. In the night, they must have floated away. I sigh, and search the pack of cigarettes in vain for one last smoke. I gather what's left of my supplies and start my way back to town.

Turning one last time, I look back at the monster, lying at the center of my makeshift camp. This isn't like one of those horror movies, though. The monster doesn't rise up for one last scare. It just lies there in a puddle of its own blood, sick and shit, waiting to start the decomposition process.

I think about how cool our younger selves would think this is. I smile when I think of us, riding bikes to the bluff to look at the town. I smile thinking about the times we had growing up. The jokes. The awkward times. I think of you and how lucky I was to have you in my life.

I think about how we'll always have this. The monster. The blood. The woods.

Cultural Appropriation or Beautiful Love

I think it's been about three decades since I died. That may be wrong. I remember being in my hotel room, watching the news here in Shimokitazawa that the Berlin wall was being torn down. That was after dinner at the restaurant in the lobby and trying urchin for the first time. I figured "When in Rome," and tried raw fish. While the news played, I drifted off to sleep, in anticipation of returning home to New York the following morning. After a long flight, of course.

Business had gone swimmingly here, contracts were signed. The salarymen who took me to dinner toasted our companies' unified efforts to renovate sections of Shimbashi and Asakusa. It was an exciting time for me. Lots of money rolling in. Lots of trips to Japan on the horizon.

Until the embolism popped in my brain while I slept.

Now, I wander the streets of Shimokitazawa, soaking in the sights. Forever. I always thought that when we died, we'd get to travel through a light-tunnel or something and I'd get to see my dog Gary again. And my grandparents. But instead, I'm stuck in a city where I don't speak much of the language, even after thirty years of eavesdropping on conversations and watching people navigate their lives. I've listened to thousands of breakfast, lunch, and dinner orders. Watched thousands of American movies with Japanese subtitles at the bottom. Japanese movies with American subtitles, too.

There's an old movie theater that went up about five years before I got to Japan, and it has stood the test of time. It plays the classics. *Blade Runner*, *The French Connection*, and more. All in English with Japanese subs. I go just about every night. The smell of the popcorn is amazing, but I can't eat any of it. I can only just barely even touch it or make it move. I'm getting better at that.

I find myself exploring the shops of Shimokitazawa. Tea shops, video game stores, record stores, the same kind of places I liked when I was back home in New York. My favorite shop is KitKat Records in the heart of the city. They have a great selection of records, but most importantly, they close at five in the evening, which lets me work on touching things without drawing attention. I can put on records and play them over the speakers of the store before I go down the street to the movies.

KitKat is also my favorite because of Manami. She started working at KitKat about ten years ago, when she was in her late teens. She's since gone to college, graduated, and become the manager/co-owner of the store. She started getting her degree in art, then changed to business management after her dad came into the store and talked her out of following her artistic inclinations and focusing on something "more real."

Manami introduced me to new bands and music I never heard before. When she's closing up, she'll put on albums like *Trouble Will Find Me* or *Antics* or *Oracular Spectacular*. She bobs her head, her dark hair dangling in her perfect face. I didn't come to Japan to fall in love. I certainly didn't come here to die. But that's what happened.

I find myself walking with Manami back to her apartment. I talk to her. Sometimes it seems like she can hear me. She'll smile after I say something funny, or sometimes I'll see her expression change as if thinking about something I said that may be profound or stupid. I never can tell the difference.

I've never been in her apartment. That just seems creepy, even to a ghost. I imagine she has cool band posters, candles, incense, and other cool stuff all over the place. Different than my apartment back home in the city. A cold, open space without much personality to it. Now, all of Shimokitazawa is my apartment. Cool vibes and warmth everywhere, even down darkened alleys where stray cats look for food and nocturnal proclivities sometimes go awry.

I stand outside Manami's apartment, and look down, noticing she's dropped a small piece of red paper. I pick it up, failing the first couple times, and tuck it in my jacket pocket. I'm permanently stuck in the clothes I died in, so I'm in my old Alan Flusser bladed drape until the end of the world, which I assume I'll also be around to see, if it ever occurs.

As I walk back to the record store, I think about how I haven't met any other ghosts in my thirty years of death. I wonder if I'm the only one. I pass by a group of salarymen partying at a local bar not far from the record store, and smile, hoping they're enjoying themselves. There's no such thing as jealousy once you've passed away. I don't feel sadness or regret or frustration. Loneliness, I suppose.

I enter the record store through the back alley door, and put on a Blue October album. I've grown to like these guys a lot since dying. It takes a lot of energy to put the record on, and I sit on the counter of the record store and think about how with the place so dark, it'd be pretty spooky if I wasn't already a ghost haunting the joint.

Remembering the paper in my pocket, I take it out and unfold it. A wave of what first feels like panic rushes over me when I see what's written on it. I look at the mirror behind the register, then at the paper again.

On the red paper, Manami has drawn a picture of me. My suit. The dopey grin I have on when I see her. My terrible mustache. I recognize the Kanji written on the paper as "I see you."

Take Only What You Need

I was dreaming about the *Care Bears* when my mom ran, screaming, into my bedroom the night we fled the house. I was floating on a cloud with Lionheart, who was my favorite because he wasn't a bear at all, but a lion, obviously. We were singing, eating pizza, and going to a playground that floated in the sky, but I never made it there because mom woke me up, screaming that we needed to "get out of here."

Half asleep, my mom covered my eyes with her jacket, as I carried my stuffed Lionheart doll down the long staircase in the house. I heard noises. Glass breaking, the sound of wind blowing, wood creaking, doors slamming. I heard the heavy stomps of what I thought was my father in the attic above us, but only as an adult, and after having had countless therapy sessions with four different analysts, only now realize that it wasn't dad at all.

When I got to the bottom of the staircase, I tripped, and when I looked up, I saw the wrought-iron chandelier swaying, the lightbulbs on it flickering, casting shadows all over the entryway to the house, and at the top of the landing. Shapes and figures emerged in the darkness and I didn't know who they were, and when I squinted to see through the combination of sleepiness and confusion, they didn't have any features. Just shapes in the minimal light, cast in total shadow.

My mom reached for me to help me up, but something grabbed her by the hair and pulled her backward, halfway up the stairs we just came down. I screamed and backed into the corner of the foyer, watching in fright as my mom struggled with something that simply wasn't there. I watched as something pulled her by her hair up a few more steps, until she was able to rip herself free.

"Teddy, run! Go outside!" mom screamed at me, but when I grabbed the doorknob, it felt hot, and twisted in my hand without me turning it. Mom eventually met me at the door and tried to break it down, but it didn't work.

"Where's daddy?" I asked, shouting over the noise and animation of the house.

Mom didn't answer. She kept trying to break the door down. I looked back at the chandelier, still swaying. Eventually, it broke free and smashed to the ground, sending metal and glass everywhere.

We ran to the back door, through the kitchen and laundry room. Locked, we struggled with the door, until finally, mom got it open and we darted out the back, into the yard. Pausing a moment, mom looked at the house and saw a shadow in the attic window. The shape of a man stood there, watching us, his hand pressed to the window.

"Stay here, do not go back in there," mom shouted before sprinting back into the house, the back door slamming shut behind her.

One of the side windows of the house exploded outward, sending glass everywhere and causing me to jump. Clutching Lionheart tighter, I was just barely able to track my mom through the house, room to room until she made it to the door to the attic, which was in the guest bedroom. Waiting for what seemed like forever, I heard her scream, watched the window in the attic crack from something being slammed against it, and closed my eyes.

After a little while, I felt a hand on my shoulder. I opened my eyes and my parents were standing there, looking white and covered in scratches and bruises. Dad scooped me up and we ran to the car. We had to cross over the broken glass, but dad didn't even flinch. He placed me in the back seat, buckled me in, and got into the passenger seat. Mom started the car and we screeched out of the driveway, down the secluded street, toward town.

I turned and looked back at the house for the last time.

The Butcher

Working for God is never easy.

When I left seminary and was placed at St. Francis in Resting Hollow, I thought small-town life would be the death of me. I'm not used to knowing all of my neighbors, or being able to walk everywhere in town. The idea of not hopping on the subway and getting to Brooklyn from my fifth floor walkup hasn't yet settled in over the six months I've been here. I miss the city, miss the people, miss the noise. Resting Hollow is quiet. Meditative. Which is good for studying the scriptures, sure, but not good if I'm craving a macchiato at two in the morning.

I find myself walking the town late at night. At first, I was pulled over by the town's overzealous police force. Being black in an affluent Hudson valley town isn't easy, but since those first couple of times being profiled by the police, I started wearing my collar when I go on my nightly constitutionals. Now, instead of being pulled over, they smile, wave, and ask if I need a ride home. Part of me wants to ask for a ride to the local bar, Fisher's, but I'm not sure how that'll look, so I just decline their offer and wave as they drive off into the night.

Grabbing my usual seat at the end of the bar, the bartender pours me a vodka and club. I'm thankful that the bars here in Resting Hollow keep city hours for the most part, mostly because of the tourist trade that helps the local economy a bit. The town has money, but is still something of a tourism spot, especially around Halloween, when the local farmers go all-out with pumpkins, corn mazes, tractor tours, etc. Local haunted houses pop up each year too, bringing thousands from the city the forty-five minute drive to our beautiful, postcard-esque hamlet.

The bartender pours me another, and I look around the bar. Some of my parishioners, lots of younger locals, some tourists I've never seen before. I finish my drink, attempt to pay my tab, but the bartender, as usual, won't let me, dismissing my attempt with "Padre, you know better."

I thank him and start out. "Need me to call you a cab, father?"

"No, thanks. The crisp air will sober me up pretty quickly, I think," I say, stepping outside.

As I start my way back to St. Francis, I notice a group of drunk tourists on the corner, shouting about one of the local haunted houses. Ignoring them, I continue down the road. I pass by another haunted attraction in town, which typically has lines down the block, and note the sounds of recorded screaming, sound effects, and horror movie music. I also pick up the faint sweet smell of pina colada, a smell added to the chemicals used to make smoke in the smoke machines in the haunted house.

I walk past a group of tourists excitedly talking about the attraction. With them is a small child, maybe seven or eight, who looks nervous, wearing an orange ski cap with a Jack O'Lantern on it. His eyes meet mine, and as I walk past, I give him a reassuring smile. He keeps his gaze on me as I walk by, further down the road.

When I get to St. Francis, I unlock the door and shoulder it to push it open, since it typically sticks. I make my way up the stairs, noting the cool breeze as I shut and lock the door behind me. I get to the clergy house, which is connected to the church itself on the north side, along the opposite street I came in from, and start to settle in for the night. I pour myself a glass of water and start sipping it, putting on some music.

I begin flipping through a copy of *Lunar Park* and start feeling tired, when suddenly I notice a knock at the door. Rising, I head over, wondering if maybe I left something behind at the bar, but when I get to the door, I peek through the window next to the door and see no one there.

"Well, that's suitably creepy," I say to myself, with a laugh. Has to be tourists, drunk teens messing with the town priest, nothing too crazy.

I return to my book and settle back in.

Another knock. Annoyed, I slip over to the door and open it. Again, nothing. "Very funny," I say, loudly, sticking my head out the door and looking down the street, both ways.

I close the door and lock it, and another round of knocking causes me to jump. I look out the window and see nothing there.

Backing away from the door, slowly, I take my phone out of my pocket and start dialing 9-1-1, but something catches the corner of my eye. Orange ski cap. Jack O'Lantern design.

"Hello?" I ask, my voice trembling.

Nothing. The child doesn't move. He's lit barely by the moonlight pouring in from the windows. His face is hidden in shadow, and he's standing completely still. I feel the air get colder, as if a window is open.

"How'd you get in here, kid?"

I start walking toward him, but pause when the smell of rotting meat fills my nostrils. I look down at the child's feet and see a swarm of bugs, worms, and centipedes crawling around.

"You're a butcher!" the child screams, his voice unnaturally guttural for his age.

Startled, I leap back. I frantically hit "send" on my phone but the call never connects. I listen and all I hear is silence.

"What do you want?" I ask, my voice trembling a bit. The insects begin swarming out from the child's feet, in all directions, seeming to multiply. The smell of rot begins to fill the room even more.

"You did this. You did this to me. To us!" the boy shouts again, stepping closer. As he lifts each foot to take a step, I see that his form is dripping with bugs. His clothes hang loose, as if there's no flesh or body to retain the shape of the child.

Overcome with terror, I run for the door and open it, dashing outside. In the cold October night, I watch as the bugs spill out of the clergy house and onto the steps and onto the sidewalk. I grab my phone and try the police again. This time, the call connects, and they arrive within five minutes.

Hours later, I'm sitting in the police station, drinking coffee, having recounted the story twice to the tiny police force. I would be annoyed if the officers didn't believe me, but they seemed genuinely concerned. At first, I chalked this up to small-town thinking, or the need for a good scare around Halloween time, but the officers showed genuine concern for me.

"So you all believe me?"

The chief, an older man in his 60s walks over to me. "Son, there's more things in this town than you know. You only been here a short time. Why do you think we haven't had a priest settled in town for longer than a year at a time?"

"Are you saying that thing, that kid, scares priests away?"

The chief shrugs. "Something does. Resting Hollow's a good town, but a town with its own share of secrets, you know?"

I nod. The chief walks me outside. He lights a cigarette. "We got a hotel room set up for you, padre. I imagine you'll be on the phone to the diocese in the morning, askin' for a transfer."

I look up the street and see the spire of the church. "No. I don't think I will. This is my church. My town."

At the hotel, I gather some water, bless it, gather my crucifix and Roman Ritual, and call an Uber. The Uber drops me off at the church. I check my watch - three in the morning.

I walk up the steps and unlock the door to the clergy house. Stepping inside, I note the faint aroma of rotting meat, like before. My right hand clutches the holy water, while my left holds the Roman Ritual to my chest.

I begin searching the clergy house for any sign of the boy. Or the bugs. The bug boy. Whatever. As I walk, I turn on every light I possibly can, thinking of how important it is to do the opposite of every horror movie character ever. I step to the door of the actual church and open it. Looking toward the altar, I see him.

My hand fumbling for the lightswitch, I flick it, but the bulbs scattered around the church explode. The smell of rot is heavy in the air.

I begin reading from the Roman Ritual. "God, by your might, defend me, and by your name, save me. Turn back this evil upon my foes, all eyes look down upon my enemies."

"Enemies ..." the boy hisses. "You are the butcher!"

As I approach, the boy turns and I see his face, twisted in a look of extreme agony, his eyes sunken and watery. I splash the holy water upon him and continue reading from the Roman Ritual. "Save your servant who trusts in you, my God."

"Save your servant, save thy soul ..." the boy screams, his voice deepening.

"Let your mighty hand cast him from your servant, from this holy vessel," I read, loudly. I look at the floor, at the swarming bugs. Some have begun to take flight and are fluttering in my face, but I close my eyes.

"I command you, unclean spirit, whoever you are, to remove yourself from this vessel of the Lord, from this place of sanctity and purity, this sanctuary of holiness."

"Sanctity …" the boy groans, his body writhing with every splash of holy water.

"Begone and stay far from this holy place," I scream.

The boy grabs my face, getting close. His teeth are black with rot, and his eyes, milky, crusting with pus and sickness. "Father …"

I feel myself slipping into unconsciousness. As I slip backward, the boy casts his gaze skyward, his eyes going wide in terror.

When I awaken the next morning, on the floor of the church, the boy is nowhere to be found. My holy water is empty. The Roman Ritual is laying on the floor next to my rosary. I gather my items and head back into the clergy house.

When I open the door, the sunshine beams in. The smell is gone.

I walk to the fridge, grab a bottle of vodka, pour myself a glass and sit down at the kitchen table. Taking a swig, I think about what happened the night before. Sometimes working for God isn't easy.

My Indestructible Friend Steve

I met Steve in junior high. When all the elementary school kids went to the tour of Irving Junior High, the place that would be our home for the next two years as we went through those weird times of physical, mental and emotional development of seventh and eighth grade, I saw Steve standing in the field outside, staring at the sun.

It was June, and our elementary schools had just finished for the year, and this blond weirdo was just out in the field, staring directly at the sun, his eyes wide open. I walked over and introduced myself, "Hey, I'm Clark."

"I'm Steve. What school did you go to?"

"Astor, you?"

He paused a moment, staring at me. His eyes were golden, with flecks of black. In that pause, it seemed like he was staring through me, as though he was searching for the answer somewhere on my face, his eyes focused on microscopic details that only he could see.

"Kingsland. But I was only here for the last month of school. My parents move a lot," he said.

"That's cool. How come they move so much?"

Steve shrugged. "Dunno."

I looked around, thinking of something to say. "You wanna' go get a popsicle and check out the baseball field?"

"Sure!"

And with that, Steve and I ran off into a summer of adventure. I introduced him to other friends of mine, but they all had the same responses, almost like everyone was reading from a script: *He's weird. His hair is so bright. Where does he live? What do his parents do? Why's he so quiet?*

Even with all these questions people kept asking me about Steve, it didn't change the fact that we were buddies. He was funny, in a way. Talking to him made me feel smart because he didn't know a lot about Resting Hollow or New York in general, so, I got to tell him about the area all the time, and his response was always, "That's interesting, Clark, thank you for telling me that."

We went to the movies for the first time together to see *I Know What You Did Last Summer* and Steve told me he had never been to the movies before. He also never had popcorn before. He seemed fixated on watching the popcorn pop and pour out of the machine into the large glass counter.

"What's that?"

"That's popcorn, bud, you ever have it?"

At this point, I knew that Steve hadn't really had a lot of things before. He said he mostly ate vegetables, because his parents didn't think it was healthy for him to eat anything else. Steve, when he was with me, always stared at the food I ate, and at first, when I would offer him a bite of a hot dog, or a slice of pizza when my parents would get us dinner (always with a side salad for him), he would refuse, saying "Mom wouldn't want me to."

Eventually, when my dad was grilling in the backyard and Steve and I were getting out of the pool, he caved when he saw my cheeseburger. "What's that?"

"A cheeseburger, man, I won't even ask if you want to try it, I know you can't."

Steve couldn't take his eyes off the burger as I squirted ketchup on it and smothered it in pickles. Eventually, when I took a bite, he gasped.

My mouth full, I asked "What's wrong?"

He looked down at his salad. No dressing, no cheese, lettuce, tomatoes, cucumbers and carrots, courtesy of my mom.

"I would like to try your cheeseburger, if that's okay?"

I nod and hand it to him. Opening his mouth as wide as humanly possible, he took a massive bite of the burger. Ketchup and pickle juice ran down his chin, onto his still-wet chest and bathing suit.

"Well? What do you think?" I asked, waiting with bated breath.

Steve chewed for a long time, then swallowed. "This is the most delicious thing I've ever eaten."

My dad pumped his fist in celebration when he heard Steve say that. "Got another one coming up for ya', bud," he said to me and returned to the grill.

I smiled, watching Steve enjoy his first cheeseburger.

From that point forward, Steve would try new foods whenever he could. After the burger, it was popcorn, after that, pizza. Cheeseburgers were still his favorite, with pizza a very close second ("I certainly enjoy cheese, Clark," he said about the pizza).

As summer started to wrap up, Steve invited me over to his house for the first time. My parents had spoken to his parents a few times on the phone, when Steve's parents would call and thank them for making dinner or letting Steve sleep over. They were very "sweet and kind" people, according to my mom, even sending over a fruit basket a few times as a thank you for taking care of their son.

Steve never told his mother that he ate other food outside the house. He said that she wouldn't be happy to hear that, so to avoid upsetting her, he kept it between us. When I got to his house, he asked if it was okay that I eat a salad like him and I told him that after a summer of cheeseburgers and pizza, I probably *should* eat a salad, and he laughed after thinking about my joke a minute or so.

He lived in one of the larger houses on a dead-end street close to the Palisades in town. A Victorian-style home built in the 1800s, Steve's family had redecorated to make it as modern as possible inside, though the walls didn't have any pictures of their family or friends or anything on them. Radios and televisions were in every room, along with computers and other pieces of technology I couldn't recognize.

Steve's mom walked into the room. She was pretty. Pale like Steve and blond. Her eyes were the same, too. "Hello, I'm Clark."

She shook my hand and thanked me for teaching Steve so much about the town and the area in general. She also thanked me for hanging out with him and being such a "good friend" to her little boy. Something about her seemed off, but not in a bad way, just in a weird, almost "not-totally-there" kinda' way, like maybe she was tired, or didn't have much energy. Her words slurred a little bit, but just by looking at her, you wouldn't know anything was wrong, she was perfect-looking in every way, right down to her wide smile, which Steve also inherited.

I wondered what, if anything, Steve got from his dad, but apparently, Steve's dad was away on business, so it was just the three of us. Steve's mom made salads for us, which we ate, and then we went outside to set up a tent so we could enjoy the cooler summer evening, since school would be starting soon. Once we had the tent set up, Steve's mom came out with a plate of veggies for us to snack on while we relaxed in the grass outside the tent.

Looking up at the stars, Steve asked "Clark, if I moved away not long after school started, how would you feel?"

I wasn't too surprised by Steve's question, since he always asked questions about how things he did would make me feel, or how things in my life have made me feel. That was a recurring thing with Steve, understanding how people felt about things.

"I'd be sad, Steve. I'd miss you, you're my best friend," I finally said after thinking a moment.

"You'd be sad?"

I nodded. Steve was staring at me. I turned and looked at him. "Yeah, we're buddies, dude. Who else would I hang out with all the time if not you?"

"Perhaps Tim, or Lew, or James or Christopher, or other Lou --"

"I'm trying to make a point, you dork," I say, cutting him off. "You're my friend. Being friends means that when one of us goes away, the other is sad about that. You like hanging out with me, right? Going swimming? Coming over? Going to the movies? All that stuff?"

"Oh yes, very much so," Steve said, smiling.

"So, if you all of a sudden weren't doing those things anymore, wouldn't *you* feel sad?"

He thought for a moment. A long moment. He stared at me, like that day we first met, in the field at school. "Yes. There would be something missing in my life. That would make me *very* sad."

I smile and pat him on the shoulder. "That's how I'd feel, too, bud."

I'm not entirely sure, but while we watch the stars, Steve seems far off. I look at him while he's lost in thought, and think I see a tear streaking down his cheek, but I never mention it, and when we went into the tent that night, he turned the lantern off and thanked me for being his friend.

About a week later, school started. The year was mostly uneventful, with the exception of normal puberty-based things. When I told Steve about how I was starting to grow facial hair, he congratulated me and seemed genuinely happy and excited for me. "This is the start of your transformation, Clark, this is wonderful!"

Steve watched while my dad taught me to shave. "Your dad hasn't shown you how to do this, little buddy?"

"No, sir," Steve replied to my dad.

"Well, it's not very hard. Razors are pretty much fool-proof these days," dad said, lathering his face and showing us how to slide the razor up from his neck, to his cheek.

"What is 'fool-proof,' sir?" Steve asked.

"It means that you can do something without making a mistake."

"Oh. Very good."

The only time I didn't see Steve was during Christmas time. He said that he and his parents had to go visit family up north. I was worried at first, because I knew how his parents had a tendency to leave town very suddenly, because of their jobs, but, thankfully, this wasn't the case. When Steve returned, he looked like he had started puberty himself. He said it was the stress of seeing his family up north that did it.

I gave him a Christmas present that year - a VHS of *I Know What You Did Last Summer*, the first movie we saw together. When I gave him the gift, at my family's Christmas party, he nearly cried, both because he was touched that I would give him a gift, but also because his family didn't celebrate Christmas, and he didn't know to get me a gift.

"That's okay, dude, Merry Christmas," I said, hugging him.

After Christmas break, school resumed, and the entire valley was covered in a blanket of powder. It never seemed to snow on Christmas, but this year was different, and returning to school was difficult, because snow kept pouring down for days. We ended up having two snow days in a row about a week after returning to school, and during those snow days, Steve and I decided to head into the woods to explore and see if the pond had frozen over completely. Some of my friends told me it did, but I needed to see it for myself.

As we walked through the woods, Steve stared at the deer and other wildlife we found. "Why don't deer go south for the winter the way birds do?"

"I don't know, man, I wish we could go south for the winter, too," I say, tossing a snowball at him. We had already had about twenty-five snowball fights to that point in our friendship from this winter alone, so Steve was already well versed in the art of snowball warfare. As we charged through the woods, tossing snowballs of various sizes at one another, we eventually arrived at the pond and found that it had, in fact, frozen over.

"Oh wow, check it out," I said, as Steve stared in awe at the frozen pond.

"We could fill many glasses of orange water with this ice!" he exclaimed.

"Orange water" is what Steve called Kool-Aid, another delicacy I introduced him to over the summer. It had become his go-to, his addiction. He was even able to convince his mother to buy it for him, assuring her that one didn't need to add sugar to it to make it delicious. He would often sneak packets of sugar (picked up from the local diner) into the bottles of Kool-Aid packed for him by his mom.

I took a few tentative steps onto the ice. Keeping my bearings on the ice is the only thing that kept my mind off the fact that I didn't really check the thickness of the ice before stepping out. I guess because I was trying to look cool in front of Steve, who was still standing along the shore, watching me, but I didn't remember to check in the way my dad taught me. I looked at the ice beneath me and remember seeing no evidence of water moving underneath. I don't remember seeing much of anything, just thick ice, and below it, darkness.

I turned to Steve, who was still standing on the shore, watching me, a look of nervousness on his face. I waved for him to join me and shouted that the ice was fine, and reminded him to go slow.

With the speed to rival a turtle, Steve took his first step onto the ice, following my footprints in the light powder of snow that fell that afternoon after the storm that morning. I watched him as he moved, his eyes darting from his feet, the ice below, and me.

When he got closer to me, he stopped. "Clark, something's wrong, do you feel it?"

I didn't know what he was talking about. There was a breeze, but nothing as crazy as the storm that morning. Some trees were knocked down in town, and some folks lost electricity, but this wind, compared to that, was nothing.

"I don't feel anything, dude."

The tiniest sound of what I thought was a branch snapping made us both jump. I looked around at the trees lining the pond, and didn't notice anything out of the ordinary. Outside of the breeze forcing snow to whip around a bit, there was nothing.

"Clark, the ice," Steve said, looking down.

As I looked down at my feet, I noticed a crack forming between my boots, leading the few feet away to Steve. The crack continued to splinter, until finally, it was large enough to extend past Steve nearly to the shore of the pond. Without warning, the ice gave way beneath us, plunging us both into the freezing dark water.

Looking back now, everything seems clearer to me than in the moment. The one constant that I've held onto has been the feeling of the icy water. One would think the first place you'd feel the water would be your limbs, but, for me, it was in my heart. The sudden jolt of the water hitting my body sent what felt like an icicle directly into my chest, and from there, the cold radiated out.

I remember trying to pull myself up toward the ice that hadn't broken away, but the weight of my clothes was almost too much for me to maneuver. The darkness around me, and the frantic movements only helped push that electric shot of cold throughout my body. My ears began to ring. My vision was blurry from the water to begin with, but darkness began creeping in from the corners of my eyes.

A sudden jolt startled me, even from the darkness that was growing around me, I felt a hand grip the back of my jacket and in one smooth motion, I was torn from the water and slid across the ice toward the shore. My teeth were chattering, and I had to have been in shock, because once removed from the water, I had no clue what happened until Steve told me, years later.

At the hospital, Steve and I were treated for hypothermia, which was mild in my case. Steve, however was perfectly fine. When his mother arrived at the hospital and finally met my parents face to face, she didn't look happy. It was the first time I saw her without some kind of smile on her face. She actually looked prettier with a serious face on.

She collected Steve and they left as quickly as she arrived, refusing to hear the doctors' diagnosis and the events of what had happened. She was cordial and apologetic to my parents, and they kept saying they were glad that we were alright. When I finally got to go home, my parents mentioned that she seemed odd, and I agreed. "Odd, but nice," my mom said, bringing me soup.

I didn't see Steve for about two weeks after the pond. The police had gone and put up a wooden fence around the pond because of what happened, along with a sign warning people not to go on the ice. Teachers from the school came to visit me and review what I was missing, and to give me updates on what I needed to do to keep my grades up. Mild hypothermia isn't that big a deal, but my doctor thought it best to keep me out of school a little bit, considering the mysterious circumstances of how I got out of the water.

"It had to have been Steve," I told them. "He saved me."

According to my parents, and the doctors, the science didn't match up. Steve was smaller than me, and he fell into the water, too, so, it would've been impossible for him to lift me out of the water and throw me closer to shore. I told them no one else was with us, so it had to be Steve. Eventually, everyone chalked my survival up to a freak underwater current, and that was that.

When I got back to school, I joined Steve at lunch and we talked about what happened. Apparently, rumors had started in the junior high that Steve was some kind of superhero or something, and that he had, in fact, lifted me out of the water. Because of this, Steve had started being bullied by kids bigger than him, who wanted to test his "super strength" or whatever, and consequently, Steve spent the rest of the year dodging bullies and building up his cardio by running away from kids who had nothing but ill will toward the weird little kid with supposed superpowers.

When the end of the year rolled around, we spent another summer swimming, barbecuing, and being ourselves. My friends wanted to get to know Steve more, so they joined us on a lot of adventures: riding bikes to the movies, heading to the Palisades, exploring the abandoned mines, all of it. My friends all wanted to know about what happened that day at the pond, but Steve and I rehearsed our answers all the time:

I don't know.

It's kinda' a blur.

I was pushed out after Clark.

I don't know who pulled me out. I thought it was Steve, but I guess not.

On the fourth of July, Steve and I were watching the fireworks in the town square. He was staying over for the week, since his parents were out of town, and during the fireworks, he whispered something to me: "It was me."

"What? Did you fart or something?"

"No, Clark, I mean, not recently, but yes, no, I mean … at the pond. It *was* me. I wanted you to know the truth. Because you're my best friend."

I stared at him, the fireworks exploding around us. His eyes were locked on the explosions above us. "How did …"

"Let's just enjoy the fireworks for tonight."

And we did. Steve and I drank "orange water" and watched the fireworks all night. After, we slept in a tent in my backyard, told ghost stories, and fell asleep. All in all, a perfect fourth of July.

While I'm drifting off to sleep, I'm thinking that I wouldn't be here to have these perfect times with my family and my friends if Steve wasn't here. He saved my life. He pulled me out of the water. I don't know how, but he did.

The following morning, I woke up and found Steve not in the tent. I poked my head out the flap and saw him standing by the pool, staring at the sun, eyes wide open, like when I first met him at school. I stepped out of the tent and walked over to him.

I stood there watching him staring at the sun for a long time, until finally, I tapped him on the shoulder, causing him to jump. "Sorry, I thought I saw a plane or something, I was trying to find it again," he said.

His eyes were darker. He rubbed them with his fists, until finally, I noticed they'd returned to their normal (for him) color. "Wanna' go in the pool?"

And so it went. We started eighth grade the following September, had a painfully normal junior high experience, our bodies changing more and more, our friendship bonds growing closer and closer. My friends became his friends, too, but it was always me and Steve. "Here comes double trouble," my dad would say when we walked into a room.

Towards the end of eighth grade, while sitting in town eating hot dogs on a bench and watching people go about their business, Steve said a combination of words I never heard him say before: "I think I like someone, Clark."

"What do you mean 'like someone?' Like, as in *like*-like?"

He nodded. "Her name is Victoria, she was in our --"

"Victoria Katzimidis? You *like* Vicky Cats?" I chuckled at this revelation. Vicky Cats was a girl in our life science class who was obsessed with animals. Her house was filled with all kinds of pets from normal things like cats and dogs to ridiculous things like African snakes and poisonous snapping turtles, which I didn't think was a real thing, but apparently it is.

"I find her interesting. She was telling me about her pets and I went over there one evening and --"

"Wait, you went to Vicky Cats' house? When?"

"Maybe a week or so ago, Clark, why?"

"Why didn't you tell me? This is very important information, man," I said, feeling a little hurt that my best buddy didn't tell me had a bona fide date with a girl.

"She was just showing me her animals, I was there maybe two hours, I suppose," Steve said, nonchalantly. I truly don't think he had any idea how huge this was. Actually hanging out with a girl like that. Even Vicky Cats. What a world.

By the end of that summer, Vicky Cats was part of our gang. I noticed Steve acted different around her than he did with the guys.

I would always catch Steve and Vicky staring at each other whether we were eating dinner somewhere, or riding bikes, or swimming in the pool, or whatever. They were stupid for each other, and never seemed to do anything about it. Our buddies teased Steve about it, but it rolled off his back. He'd often dismiss our insults with "I can't help it, there is a feeling inside when she's around. It is an awakening."

Things like that didn't seem weird once you got to know Steve. He was an old soul. The kid had a remarkable sense of who he was, and that sense of who he was carried us through eighth grade and into the start of high school. Vicky and Steve seemed closer all the time. I even caught them holding hands at the movies once, and Steve admitted they had kissed a couple of times when he walked her home after we all hung out.

The first few years of high school were some incredibly weird times. I attempted to grow a mustache that looked completely ridiculous, and was teased mercilessly about it by everyone (including my dad). Vicky, who started as a short, chubby girl with glasses and bad clothes, suddenly changed into one of the most beautiful girls in school, but she only had eyes for Steve. Steve, meanwhile, played football and took a hit so hard, he was knocked out of his cleats. He ended up dusting himself off, re-tying his laces, and immediately got back into the game, despite his helmet being cracked. The coach just called him a "tough sonofabitch," and that was that.

Steve had changed perhaps most dramatically of all of our friends. By eleventh grade, my former shrimpy friend had grown to over six feet tall, his blond hair and perfect skin no longer looked babyish, and instead, he was often approached by girls in school. The thing was, Steve was head over heels for Vicky and had been for years.

Eventually, they got together and were officially a couple. Our friend group, over time, started including girls more and more, and I even found a main squeeze in the form of Kerry Hannigan, whose dad was chief of police and absolutely terrifying to talk to. I always imagined that he was waiting at home with a rifle and a badge ready to blow my head off, should I bring his daughter home later than the agreed-upon drop off time.

In a move I learned from my buddy Lew, I started cutting our dates short by about an hour, so Kerry and I could have some alone time, and still have enough time to get her home to dad without a problem. When I told Steve this strategy, he asked "Why would you need alone time with her? Don't you feel that when she's around, she's the only person in the entire world?"

Steve had grown into a full-blown romantic.

I started seeing less and less of Steve's mom. She was always "away on business" or "on vacation" or sometimes just "not home." My parents often wondered how Steve's parents could leave him home alone so much, but he seemed fine with it. In high school, we settled into a routine of video games on Friday nights, Saturday nights with our respective girls, and Sundays were for breakfast at the diner, sometimes with our girls, sometimes not, but always together. Steve had been the one to propose this schedule, and hosted many of the video game nights at his house, always providing plenty of snacks, drinks, and the latest games to play. How he got them without a job is anyone's guess, but nobody said anything and nobody complained.

High school eventually ended, and it was time to face the ultimate test of our young lives - college. Vicky was heading to school further upstate to be a veterinarian, while Steve was entertaining the idea of going into his family's business, allowing him to stay in town and live at home to save money while working and taking classes at the local university.

The rest of us scattered to schools all over the country. I landed in Florida, enjoying time drinking and partying at the University of St. Augustine. The group of friends stayed in touch, thanks in part to the rise of social media, but it was harder to get together as much, since we were all over the country.

Because I was in Florida, the guys came to me often, but Steve wasn't always able to get away from work and school. While we spent days on the beach as often as possible, Steve remained back north, working on his degree. He described the program he was in as "very demanding" of his free time, to the point where he and Vicky almost broke up because he wasn't able to see her as much.

He said he was glad they didn't because Vicky had become a "light" in his life that he didn't want to see go out.

Nevertheless, eventually, Steve was able to make it down to Florida with the guys to visit me. We spent a few days soaking up the sun (Steve, as usual, staring directly at the sun, no sunglasses or sunblock, yet always pale), partying, drinking, and getting wild in Florida. Steve, who had never been drunk before, found himself reeling after a particularly aggressive night of partying.

He had begun slurring his words, speaking in a language I had never heard before, but sounded close to German. Our buddy Tim asked if Steve had suddenly become a Nazi, while Lew was convinced our guy was possessed by demons, but after a while, during a particularly wild foam party at a club on the beach, Steve vanished.

We spent a good portion of the night looking for him, but he was nowhere to be found, and people at the club had no memory of who we were talking about. It was almost as if Steve, who had been drinking for about six hours straight, just up and vanished.

After about two hours of trying to track down our friend, we eventually returned to my dorm room and fell asleep in various positions all over the tiny room. I was able to rest maybe five minutes on the couch, until I decided I couldn't leave Steve out there, so I headed back out, on my own, my booze-soaked mind starting to pull itself back together.

We had checked every bar, called every hospital, every doctor's office, all over the place, but nothing. I walked up and down the streets, looking for him, thinking I'm seeing him around every corner, in every bar. The hospitals would've had to tell me if a guy matching his description came in, right? They wouldn't lie about that kind of thing, I hoped.

Eventually, I found myself about a mile away, outside the hospital near the university. In a pile next to the sign saying "St. Augustine Hospital - *A Place for Wellness*" is Steve. He was slumped in a pile, his clothes torn on the side, but otherwise fine. A small puddle of radioactive-looking green puke was at his feet. I helped him up and together, we hailed a cab and headed back to the dorm.

Once there, I tucked him into my bed and sat on the floor next to him, the couch now occupied by both Tim and Lew, who were spooning. Steve was muttering things in that same language as earlier in the night, only now it was slower and more slurred. I couldn't make much of it out at the time.

The next morning, the rest of the gang went out for breakfast, but I stayed behind with Steve, to make sure he was feeling better. When he awoke, he drew back the shades on the window, bathing the room (and himself) in sunlight. The light woke me up and I asked him how he was feeling.

"I'm well, Clark, how are you?"

"Hungover. Tired. Where did you go last night?"

That's when I noticed his ribs. In the spot where his shirt was torn, there were pieces of glass, metal; and rocks stuck to his skin. I reached up and plucked a piece of glass out of his side, and he stared at it, surprised.

"Dude, what happened to you?"

He and I started pulling pieces of metal off his skin. There were no cuts, no bruises, just multiple small pieces of glass, metal; and rocks stuck to his flesh, which was oddly cool. The pieces of metal, glass, and more left small indentations in his skin, which immediately re-shaped itself back to normal upon removal, like his skin was made of silly putty or something.

"You mustn't tell the others, if I tell you, okay?"

I nodded. Steve went on to tell me that he got separated from the group and found himself in the middle of the street. After walking for a good ten minutes or so, he was struck by a truck.

"Jesus, man," I said, legitimately terrified.

"The people got out and helped me into the bed of their truck, and dropped me off outside the hospital, which is where you found me," Steve said, peeling his shirt off and tossing it in the garbage. We finished plucking the metal and glass from his body, and I gave him one of my school shirts to wear.

I poured us some coffee and stared at him while we both drank. "Steve, how could you survive that? This isn't the first time something like this happened to you."

"Time passes quickly, doesn't it?"

I nodded, "It does."

"When you found me in that field, all those years ago, before junior high, do you remember what I was doing?"

"You were staring at the sky."

"Right. I'm not from Resting Hollow, at least, not originally," Steve said.

"I know, you moved there a little bit before school started."

"No, you misunderstand me. Earth isn't my home. I'm a guest here. A very lucky one at that. Resting Hollow gave me the life I didn't expect to ever have," Steve told me, his eyes intense and bright.

"What do you mean?"

"Where I am from, we don't have a sun. Where I'm from, the planet was plunged into darkness because of rampant consumption and corporate greed," Steve said, his voice shaking a bit. "I was only a child, but even then, I had records to guide me and inform me of what my world was like before I came to Earth, came to Resting Hollow."

"You're an alien?"

"Not like in *Predator* or anything, no, not in that sense. I am very much an alien, meaning, I am a being from another *place*."

I stared at him, thinking he was messing with me. If it was any of the other guys, I would've laughed and probably thrown a beer can at them, but Steve was never one to joke or tease, so his words held water. He was my best friend, after all, and best friends don't lie to each other.

"Why didn't you ever tell me?"

"Is it an easy conversation to have? 'Yes, hello, my name is Steve and I am from another place not of your understanding or ability to travel to, would you be my friend, Earth-boy?'"

I laughed at that one. "That's fair."

"I am telling you this now because you are my closest friend. Vicky is my love, but she doesn't know about this. I am a refugee here, and I've seen my time with you and the others as a privilege, I wish to remain my normal self," he told me, his voice desperate.

"So you *did* save me at the pond all those years ago."

He nodded. "I couldn't let my best friend die. Mother wasn't happy that I exposed myself in that way, but, she got over it when I explained how much you mean to me, Clark."

Touched by his words, I stepped close and hugged Steve. "You're my best friend too, pal. Your secret is safe with me, it's not my story to tell."

"Thank you, you're a true friend."

Our friends returned and saw us hugging. Suffice to say, that was enough to keep the conversation light and completely off the track of Steve being an alien, and what happened the night before. We told them that he stumbled in after meeting a group of girls who wanted to party with all of us, but he couldn't find us, so he hung out with them instead. The guys bought it, they had no reason not to.

Friendships are a weird thing. We get older. We have children. The world changes. People change. Our friend-group hasn't. Mostly thanks to our indestructible friend, Steve. He has always made the effort to keep us all together. Every Christmas, every New Year's, every fourth of July, every Thanksgiving, Steve is there to host us at his beautiful home, the home he grew up in.

He would later tell me that his mother returned to their world and never came back. He told me that he took that to mean the door was closed and he would never see her again. In high school, we were obsessed with girls, parties and sports, and there was Steve, secretly mourning the loss of his mother. Lost to a place he could never return.

At Steve and Vicky's wedding, we gathered to celebrate our weird little friend and the love of his life. The one who came to us from another place and made our lives so much better than they ever could have been. The one who became a fixture at family gatherings. The "nice" and "polite" boy who gave us so much, who genuinely wanted to understand us, not only as humans, but as friends. The one who discovered love at an early age and held onto it for so long.

As I toasted our friend, as his best man, I saw Vicky smile and squeeze his hand. Later, Steve told me that he finally told Vicky the truth about who he was. Terrified at first, she realized quickly that it didn't matter and that he was the shy boy she fell in love with in junior high. Vicky became Resting Hollow's top veterinarian, and Steve, sneaky devil he is, went into teaching physics at the college he got his doctorate from.

We all still gather, when called home by our friend Steve. Over two decades of friendship, separated by time and distance, and we still share our lives with one another. There is something otherworldly in that.

Kiwi

I made my first doll when I was in middle school. Back then, it was just an arts and crafts project my mom arranged for me one day after school. It took a while to sew and stuff the doll, but in the end, after a few days, I had my own Raggedy Ann knockoff. I'd always been "crafty" as my friends called it, so when the opportunity to create artisan dolls and figures to sell online presented itself, I jumped at the chance.

I was working at the coffee shop and taking classes at the university, and dating the man who'd eventually become my husband, so having the extra income from selling handmade dolls online would be nice. Thankfully, because I had so much practice for so many years, I'd become pretty good at it, so, my dolls ranged anywhere from $25 to $650 a pop. Custom dolls were the most popular orders I received early on, and because my sewing skills progressed to the point where I could bang out a doll in about a day, the only problem became sourcing clothes and painting the faces. All the dolls have porcelain faces, and thus, require extensive painting.

The first time the mailman delivered a huge box of unpainted doll heads to my house, my mom freaked out, since I was still living at home. "You gotta' spend money to make money," she said, after a while, and she helped me with those first few orders. Arts and crafts was our thing, and we always had a fun project to work on. We would spend hours working on projects, drinking jasmine tea and listening to Four Seasons records, mom taking the occasional break to glide around the room, pretending to dance with my dad, like at their wedding so many years ago. Dad passed away when I was in high school, a car accident coming home late from work one night.

The process to have a doll made is fairly simple. There are multiple choices on my site that afford parents the option to upload a photo of their daughter or whatever reference they'd like me to use in crafting a doll. Most parents want a doll that resembles their child, that's the most common request. Some will have dolls made of family members, some famous people, etc. The weirdest request I ever got was for a doll of Muammar Gaddafi, from a repeat customer in Finland. I don't ask questions, I just do the job.

My business goes through periods of slowdown, typically in the summer. Christmas is insane, though, so, that carries me through. There's no shortage of little girls with moms who have the disposable income to drop a few hundred bucks on handpainted dolls for their kids. American Girl Dolls are great and all, but they don't offer the kind of one-to-one attention and craftsmanship that I can.

About a year after I got married, I was over mom's house, drinking tea and listening to The Four Seasons croon "My Eyes Adored You" with mom and working on a doll for a little girl in

New Zealand whose mother found my website through some kind of "mommies of Facebook" group posting. Mom had been complaining about indigestion all day, and the tea, which usually helped, wasn't working. The doll was nearly finished, I just had to paint the features and re-sew a couple spots on the outfit the girl's mother chose.

While working on the doll, my mother placed her hands flat on the table, looked around the room, confused, and fell over. I jumped out of my seat and went to her, but she couldn't say anything, and by the time the ambulance arrived, she was gone. A massive heart attack, the doctors said. I took some time off from making dolls after that. The pain and memory of working on them with mom was just too fresh in my mind. I started attending grief counseling meetings at the local churches and schools, but nothing really helped until I started seeing a therapist one on one.

Over time, I started working on the dolls again, and was thankful to reconnect with the memory of my mother through my business. I never sold the doll to the New Zealand customer, instead making an entirely new one and shipping it for free after cancelling her initial order. Though it was weeks behind the promised delivery date, the customer was happy and offered to pay anyway, which I refused. I decided to name the original, unfinished doll, Kiwi.

Kiwi sits, mostly finished, on a shelf in my sewing room, which is littered with fabrics, doll heads, tiny outfits, and more. My husband busts my chops from time to time about straightening up, but I tell him that it's all "organized chaos" and that I know where everything is, which of course is not true at all, but it sounds good enough that he doesn't bother me about it too much.

One night, when I was working on a Robert E. Lee doll for a client in California, Kiwi moved. I was tired, having been sewing all day, and sourcing prints and patterns for another doll that I'd have to work on the following week, so I chalked it up to being stressed and exhausted. When Kiwi moved again the following night, I tried to record a video of it with my phone, but it stopped right as I hit the record button.

When I told my husband what happened the second night, he rolled his eyes. We've never been the types to believe in this stuff, so it's normal that he'd have this reaction. Sure, we've seen the movies and stuff, so if the doll was actually moving by itself, then clearly, the first course of action should be to burn the doll, hire a priest, move out of the house (or burn it down, too), and flee to another part of the country or a new country altogether. That's not what we did, though. Instead, in order to prove to him that the doll moved, I rearranged my workspace so I could watch Kiwi while working on other dolls.

That night, Kiwi didn't move, but over the course of the next week, Kiwi moved three times, from simple movements like lifting her arm a bit to turning her head or raising her foot forward off the shelf. Kiwi was an expensive doll, made with movable arms and legs connected to joints on a porcelain body. As I said, very expensive with extensive clothing and appliances that needed to be worked on that I would never get to.

Each time Kiwi moved and I caught it, I kept thinking about why it was happening. I started researching hauntings and the causes behind dolls being haunted, and a lot of it had to do with the dolls being a "conduit" for activity due to them essentially being representative of a human being. Or, as some people point out online, ghosts are just dickheads and like to possess things made for the comfort of children. Whatever the reason, Kiwi kept moving, little by little, on her own, for weeks.

While eating breakfast one Saturday, my husband said something that changed our lives. "You know, I was looking things up on eBay last night and I found listings for haunted dolls. You should do that."

"What? Sell Kiwi? You know I can't do that, that's the last doll mom and I worked on together," I said, almost offended by the idea of selling it.

"No, no, not that doll, but like, other ones. Weirdos buy these things all the time, I looked it up and found a bunch of articles about it. You have a bunch of dolls that didn't work out, right? Ones that are busted, or the paint was messed up, or whatever, why not add a layer of dirt to them, creep them up a bit, and sell them on eBay as 'haunted' or 'cursed' or whatever?"

I sat there and thought about it. "I've got about two dozen dolls that were either busted in some way, returned, or whatever. I could definitely do something with those."

"Here, look," he said, showing me a few of the listings on his phone. The prices were around what I was charging, and some of the dolls were in way worse shape than anything I had lying around, waiting to be cannibalized for parts. "We'd just have to come up with a bullshit ghost story to go with them. Maybe create a fake eBay account to sell them? Just a thought."

With that, the seed was planted. Over the next few days, I created the eBay account, went through the box of leftover or broken dolls, added some grime and dirt, re-painted a few (while still working on my regular orders), and started listing them. When I got to the item description screen, I found it hard to put together the stories of these particular dolls. Because I had so many listings of "haunted" dolls, I had to start with the basic premise that I was a collector of haunted artifacts and had to pare down my collection.

From there, I created names and stories that varied from discoveries in attics of old Victorian homes on Long Island to crawl spaces in Louisiana. Witches to voodoo priests to cursed men and demons, all things pulled from the movies I'd been watching my entire life, but with the details changed enough that they might be passed off as original.

About two days after listing the first three dolls, I sold one for $280. The doll really was just a blond girl from Kentucky whose mother failed to pay for the doll after commissioning it for $400. I rubbed a layer of dirt on the doll, and added some really great, high quality, homemade "blood" to her once-white dress (the most popular color for moms in the Midwest buying dolls for their daughters, by the way). The "blood," for the record, is just corn syrup mixed with red food coloring, with a tiny bit of clear dishwasher soap in case the client wants the blood washed out.

My husband joked that I should use real blood because "what if one of these nuts who buys a doll has it tested? Wouldn't they be disappointed?"

I must have been crazy, but I gave it some thought. From that point on, I decided not to include any more blood on the dolls themselves, just the illusion of it in the painting of fingernails and splotches on their feet. The other two dolls from the initial three sold shortly after, one for $120, the other for a surprisingly high $400, even though the porcelain head was cracked in places. In the product description for that one, I noted that the doll had been discovered in a New York City loft, tied to the wall, as part of a potential satanic ritual.

Considering my cost per doll head ranges between $1 and $4, with the overall cost per doll being somewhere around $20 to make, netting a clear $100 or more in profit is pretty great, especially with dolls that are essentially broken or otherwise useless.

After the sale of the third doll, I had slacked off in terms of working on additional "haunted" dolls for the eBay store. Messages began coming in from my buyers, thanking me and telling me about the activity that had started in their homes upon arrival of the dolls. I showed my husband the messages and he laughed. We both did, really.

The idea of these perfectly normal (albeit fucked up looking) dolls causing paranormal activity in these buyers' houses was too ridiculous to fathom. I would often respond with something simple like "Thank you for letting me know and thank you for your purchase, your feedback means a lot."

Over time, I continued getting more messages about haunted dolls, asking if any more were going to be for sale, and I replied that more were in the process of being listed, which wasn't true, but I had to tell potential buyers something. After a few weeks, I had enough free time to work on another round of "haunted" dolls, this time listing six, and within days, all were purchased for their asking prices. The lowest doll sold for $200, and the highest, $650. Over a thousand dollars for a day of work, uploading and adjusting old ghost stories enough to make them modern or "original."

More positive feedback. In the meantime, my regular doll business was still going, so I focused on those, too. Recruiting my husband, I would work on the dolls, he would write the "story" behind them. It was a good system, since my husband is a bigger creep than I am, the stories veered away from being pastiches of traditional horror tales to becoming more detailed and elaborate and truly works of original fiction.

The only time I had to reign my husband in was when he tried to tell a story of a particular doll that was found in the sewers of NYC that was part of some kind of underground society's ritualistic sacrifice. "This one is just plain ridiculous," I told him.

All the while, Kiwi remained on the shelf, moving, sometimes imperceptibly over the course of a few hours. One night, while I worked on a doll for a girl in Delaware, Kiwi leapt off the shelf, landing at my feet, a good seven feet from where she sat.

Picking the doll up, I noticed how she felt warm to the touch. I checked the heating duct beneath the shelf, but it wouldn't be putting out hot air in the summer, so I checked the other dolls, too, and unsurprisingly, they were room temperature.

Suddenly, the radio clicked on, at first static, then once the static faded, Franki Valli's high register slowly faded in. *I worked my fingers to the bone, made myself a name. Funny I seemed to find that no matter how the years unwind, still I reminisce about the girl I miss and the love I left behind.*

I placed Kiwi back on the shelf and walked over to the radio, flipping it off. Shaking my head at how weird that was, I flipped the lightswitch and left the room, heading to bed.

That night, I dreamt of my mom. We were sitting at the kitchen table at her house, listening to records, and working on the dolls. She looked happy, we were drinking our usual tea, and chatting. Nothing more eventful than that.

When I woke up the following morning, I was alone in bed and the smell of jasmine filled the room. My husband had left for work, and the house was quiet.

I spent the day sourcing parts, and working on designs for dolls, sketching rough ideas and using colored pencils to get a rough idea of how the doll would look, once finished. While sketching outside, enjoying the warm summer day, I caught a glimpse of the curtain moving upstairs in my sewing room. Putting my sketchbook down, I headed upstairs to check, and when I opened the door, Kiwi was on the floor again, this time next to my workspace chair.

The curtain was perfectly still, and there was no breeze in the room.

I picked her up, and like before, noted how warm she felt. This time, I carried her down the stairs and outside with me, while I worked. A few more orders came in on eBay, since I listed a few more dolls, and while checking my feedback, I watched as Kiwi's head moved to face a small group of birds in the yard.

Over time, the more I kept Kiwi with me, the more she would move. She never got up and tap danced or anything like that, but her head would move, her eyes would blink, and she would move her arms more. Sometimes I noticed that she was pointing at something in particular, sometimes my keys if I was looking for them, sometimes the television remote, most of the time, my phone.

Every night, I would place her back on the shelf in the sewing room before heading to bed. My husband thought it was strange at first, that Kiwi would just be sitting in the kitchen, or sometimes in the living room while we relaxed at the end of the day. "That thing's not coming into the bedroom, kid," he told me, and I agreed. The bedroom was literally the last place Kiwi needed to be.

Kiwi just became part of our routine. When I told friends about how she moved and what I had experienced, they all thought I was going through some kind of mental break, but when my husband confirmed it and I showed them video of her moving, they changed their tune. Eventually, a friend of mine convinced me to set up a website solely for the haunted dolls part of my business, considering my sales hadn't slowed down.

The main problem was, I was running out of dolls from my discard pile to make "haunted," so I had to start using new dolls. The process was roughly the same, and my creep of a husband was never short on ideas for backstories, so on we rolled. I even used a video of Kiwi moving on the website to add some legitimacy to my sales.

That's when things got stranger. I started getting emails asking if Kiwi was for sale. I would email back and politely refuse, thanking the person for their interest, but Kiwi was one of the few dolls that wasn't for sale. Often, I would recommend another doll, which would be purchased a day or so later, but the emails didn't stop.

At first, it was easy to refuse an offer for Kiwi, because after all, Kiwi was the only potentially legitimately haunted doll in my home. There was something special about that, and because of the comfort I felt having her around, the idea of selling her just didn't feel right.

Months went by, and the "haunted" doll aspect of my business began to catch up to the regular doll business. To cover my tracks on both fronts, I only shipped the dolls through a separate service, using a friend's address in another town, so people wouldn't be able to connect the dots as to whether or not the same dollmaker from Resting Hollow, NY, was making cursed objects and selling them online. From what I could tell, this wasn't exactly *illegal*, just unethical.

I would update the site regularly, with more videos and photos of Kiwi moving or whatever the case may be. I guess because I felt that Kiwi was drawing in more hits to the site, I felt she lent credibility to what I was doing. This didn't help stop the emails coming in offering to buy her.

Eventually, an email came in from a guy who contacted me a couple times previously. The first time, he offered $1,000 for Kiwi. The second time, $3,000. I would reply with essentially the same thing each time, that Kiwi was too special to me to sell, and that I appreciated his efforts and hope he browses the other dolls in the collection.

His latest email read essentially the same as the previous ones. He was always very pleasant, a widower in North Carolina who had bought one of my other dolls before, and swore there was activity going on in his kitchen each night because of it. His latest offer for Kiwi was $15,000.

My jaw dropped when I saw the offer. I paced around the sewing room, looking at the laptop screen, looking at Kiwi, back and forth. Eventually, I called my husband at his job and told him how much this guy was offering for Kiwi and he immediately said "Sell it."

I didn't know what to do. Kiwi was special to me in a way no other doll had been since I started my business. Things were actually happening with her around, she would actually move, this wasn't a trick or a made-up story like the ones my husband was coming up with for our "haunted" doll collection. On the other hand, $15,000 would help around the house, for sure.

I emailed back and let the gentleman know that I would think about his offer. He replied almost instantly that he appreciated it.

The next day, I talked it over with my husband, and again, he indicated that he felt I should sell Kiwi. While yes, it's fantastic that there's actual activity going on with the doll, at the end of the day, $15,000 is a lot of money and could help us more than a haunted doll ever could.

And so it was. I agreed to the payment, which was sent via Paypal immediately, packaged Kiwi up, and shipped her to North Carolina. Weeks passed. Sales via the website began to slow down, both for the "haunted" dolls *and* the regular ones. Christmas wasn't super far off, so I was preparing for the onslaught of gift orders, so the tapering off of sales before didn't bother me much, and I didn't think too much about it. Plus, the sale of Kiwi was a nice buffer.

On Christmas Eve, I received an email from Kiwi's owner. I didn't get to read it until my husband and I got home from his office Christmas party, and even then, I was a little tipsy, so, upon reading it the first time, it didn't make much sense to me. In the email, the buyer indicated that the activity had only ramped up since Kiwi arrived. What was once a fairly innocent haunting in his home turned into a full-scale attack on a daily basis.

He had tried everything, priests, science, whatever one is supposed to do to rid themselves of "evil spirits," apparently. Nothing worked. Kiwi and the doll he purchased previously had gone too far, apparently even killing his cat, Waffles, in the night. I decided that the buyer was only trying to add to the mythology of my items, so, I thanked him for his email, and asked what he would like me to do about the disturbances.

Usually pretty responsive, the buyer didn't write back until the day after Christmas. In that follow-up email, he asked if he could return Kiwi for what he paid, no questions asked. I talked to my husband about returning the money and his response was "I figured it would be too good to be true. It's not like we spent the money, right? It's your business, whatever you want to do, I back your move."

I didn't get a chance to respond until the next day, but when I turned the computer on, my husband called from the living room that a package had arrived. When I went into the living room, he handed me a knife to cut the package open, and when I did, I saw Kiwi's half-finished face staring back at me. I checked the box, no note, nothing from the buyer, not even a return address.

"Didn't you ship this from the service?" my husband asked.

"Of course. Why?"

"Then how would the buyer know to ship it to our house?"

I held Kiwi in my hands. Warm as always.

That night, I inspected Kiwi closer. There were flecks of red on her dress. Her hands, too. Her unfinished face had tiny flecks of red on them. Her dress and shoes had gotten dirty with grit and grime. She smelled like jasmine.

I never heard from the buyer again, and when I tried to process the refund, Paypal couldn't verify the man's account, so the money never transferred, it just sat in my account for months until eventually, I transferred it to my bank account.

Sales picked up again. Kiwi returned to the shelf in my sewing room, watching me work.

She's still there.

My eyes adored you like a million miles away from me,
You couldn't see how I adored you,
So close, so close and yet so far.

What Would Batman Do?

I had been sent to principal Himbry's office a few times before, but this time was different. While I sat outside, my feet dangling a few inches above the floor, I thought about what got me there in the first place. Throwing half a bologna sandwich at Timothy Buckner because he said my sneakers were stupid-looking seemed like a good idea at the time. He had it coming. Timothy always had it coming. To tell someone their sneakers were stupid was a put-down, and if I know anything, I know that it's not okay to put someone down, so I did what I thought was best.

I thought about my parents and what they'd do this time. Take away TV privileges? Take my Super Nintendo away? Whatever the case, it was worth it to see that greasy meat slam into Timothy's dumb gap-toothed face. I didn't think I'd turn into such a vengeful little prick in fifth grade, but hey, I guess it happens. I imagined myself a budding Batman-to-be, having spent the majority of my life reading Batman comics and fashioning capes from towels and bedsheets around the house (mostly when my parents weren't watching). Batman became a vengeance and justice-fueled buttkicker when he was a kid, so I guess I saw that as my life's mission, too, only without losing my parents in the process.

When the principal's door opened, a girl I had seen in school a few times stepped out. She had her head down, her hair in a ponytail, and red cheeks, like she'd been crying. She was wearing a Power Rangers sweatshirt and green gym shorts, black Converse sneakers, and I asked who her favorite Ranger was as she walked by, but she didn't answer me. I remember wondering what she must have done to get the principal so upset that she'd be crying.

I sat down in the overstuffed leather chair in the principal's office and he started in with the troublemaker stuff and why I would do such a gross thing to another student, and how it didn't matter what Timothy said about my sneakers, I still shouldn't throw things at people. I replied that it was unfair that Timothy wasn't in trouble, too, because, after all, this was entirely his fault for opening his dumb buck-toothed mouth about my sneakers.

"Two days detention, Charles, after school. Reporting to Mrs. Leshaw," the principal said, writing a few notes in a large book on his desk. With that, I was released from his company and sent back to class. That night, he would call my parents and tell them what happened, and when they'd found out, my mom would ground me for the weekend.

When Monday rolled around, I served my first day of detention after school with Mrs. Leshaw, who secretly I was in love with. I had her in fourth grade and when I showed up for detention, she remembered how I was "such a nice young man," and that she couldn't believe I was in detention. I told her it wasn't the first time that year, and probably wouldn't be my last.

She smiled and laughed when I said that and I immediately started planning our wedding. During my fantasizing about Mrs. Leshaw, I noticed the girl from the principal's office walking outside. The principal came up behind her and walked next to her, talking about something. She stood there and talked with him a bit, fidgeting with her backpack and books in her hands. The principal touched her cheek, smiled, got in his car and left the school.

The next day at lunch, I saw her again, sitting by herself. I didn't know what to say to her, so I just watched her like a creep. She seemed to not notice the other kids in the lunchroom, and they didn't seem to notice her, either. She was wearing her Power Rangers sweatshirt again, same Converse sneakers, too.

After school, I sat with Mrs. Leshaw while she graded papers, and helped her put them in alphabetical order. She thanked me for my help and told me that I could sneak out early and it would be "our little secret," so when I finished alphabetizing the papers, I left detention, thinking about how much Mrs. Leshaw was in love with me.

I used to take the back way out of the school, by the gym, because my house was just over the fence and through the neighborhood bordering the school. When I turned the corner down the hallway, toward the back of the school, I saw the principal and the same girl from earlier in the day sitting on a bench outside the gym. The principal turned and spotted me, and I saw his hand suddenly move from her stomach to his knee.

I walked past slowly, and he waved, his face red, and her eyes down on the floor, her ponytail slung over her shoulder. She was crying. "Have a good day, now," principal Himbry said. I waved back and ran out the back door of the school, hopping the fence next to the soccer field.

That night, I was in my room reading Batman comics and thinking about what I saw earlier that day. I played the moment over and over in my head, trying to figure out if it was actually what I thought I saw. *Why did principal Himbry have his hand on her stomach? Why was he so nervous? Why didn't she look at me when I walked by? Who was that girl?*

Wednesday is possibly the worst day ever invented, and so it must follow that Wednesdays in school are somehow even worse. Between the quizzes for both science and English, and dealing with Timothy again (this time I slugged him in the arm for mouthing off about Mrs. Leshaw), I found myself in the principal's office, only this time, instead of listening to him yell at me about hitting a gap-toothed jerk who totally deserved it, I would ask him about the crying girl on the bench outside the gym yesterday after school.

Principal Himbry was five minutes into his tirade when I blurted out "Who was that girl on the bench with you yesterday?"

He paused. Himbry was a big man. Fat, but with some muscle to him, too, like a lumberjack or something. He looked like a cross between John Candy and the Incredible Hulk. "What girl?"

"The one crying on the bench with you after school. You were touching her, I saw it."

With that, principal Himbry recoiled and leaned against his desk. "You didn't see anything, there was no girl."

Staring at him, I said "I know what I saw, principal Himbry."

He just stared at me, sweat forming on his brow. "How about this time, I let you off with a warning? Detention clearly isn't working with you, so, maybe we change our tactics, right? That's what they teach you in school when it comes to discipline in an educational setting."

"The 'tough love' approach?"

"You could call it that, Charles, sure," he said. "You're free to go."

I stood up and left his office, feeling uneasy at his sudden change in tactics. I may have only been a kid, but even then, I knew something was up. I wondered if this new change in approach would mean I could beat up Timothy Buckner whenever I wanted, or if it truly was only this one time. I also needed to know who that girl was. If Himbry wasn't going to tell me, I'd have to find out myself. That's what Batman would do.

That evening, I flipped through an old yearbook, still punished by my parents for the bologna incident the previous week. I checked the section of the yearbook with my classmates and didn't find her. I decided to check the other grades and when I went to the fifth graders of last year, I found her. She's a year older, which makes sense why I wouldn't know her. With her being in sixth grade, she'd be heading to junior high next year, and most of the sixth graders were too cool to socialize with us "little kids" at the time, so all of that checked out. Crystal Foster. *That's a nice name,* I thought to myself.

After finding Crystal in the yearbook, I went back to my grade and found Timothy's picture, grabbed some whiteout and covered his name. When the whiteout dried, I wrote "Fart" in its place. From that day forward, Timothy Buckner would forever be known as "Fart" in my fourth grade yearbook.

The next morning, my parents were gathered around the kitchen table, looking nervous and sad. They asked me to sit down, so I did, and my dad poured me a bowl of Captain Crunch, which I still eat to this day, even though it scrapes the roof of my mouth. "Charlie, boy, we need to talk," my dad said.

"Look, I'm sorry okay? Timothy really gets my goat, and principal Himbry said that he's going to try a different approach with me, I don't even really know what that means, so --"

"Charlie, slow down, pal," dad said, stopping me. "There's no easy way to talk about this, but, something happened last night, something happened to a girl at your school."

"What?"

"She was in sixth grade," mom started. "They found her at the quarry. It looked like she was maybe playing there and fell in."

A pit started to form in my stomach. I knew the answer to the question before I even asked "Who was she?"

"Her name was Crystal," dad said.

My parents asked if I wanted to stay home from school that day to talk about what happened and spend some time with me so I'd feel better, but I thought *what would Batman do?* and decided that going to school to gather information and watch other people deal with the news was the smarter option.

At school, people were crying, and there were flowers outside Crystal's classroom. During the day, school counselors were all over the place, talking to kids, talking to teachers. Usually, the school counselors sat in their offices doing what appeared to be nothing, but today, I guess they were useful. When I walked past Crystal's classroom, taking note of the various flowers outside, I looked inside and saw an empty desk with a bouquet on it. Crystal's teacher was talking to the students about something I couldn't make out, so I headed back to class.

When one of the counselors came to talk to me, I mentioned that I didn't really know Crystal, but I liked her Power Rangers sweatshirt and she seemed nice. I told them how I felt bad that I wouldn't get to know her better, and that I thought it was unfair that I wouldn't get to see her anymore. The counselor asked if I wanted to talk again, and I said "maybe, I guess."

That night, my punishment lifted in light of what happened, I had dinner with my parents. They seemed different, paying more attention to me. My dad wanted to go to a Yankee game that summer with me, and my mom wanted me to help her in the kitchen and garden more. I didn't understand why all of a sudden they wanted to spend more time with me when they said these things, but while lying in bed, it dawned on me that they didn't want to lose time with me the way Crystal's parents had. I remember how sad that made me feel and how I loved my parents even more for realizing that these horrible things could happen to me, too.

In school on Friday, I saw principal Himbry in the hallway talking to one of the counselors, the one who talked to me the day after Crystal died. When I walked past, Himbry's eyes locked with mine and I didn't look away. He was smiling.

Saturday evening rolled around and though it took some convincing, I got my parents to let me out of the house so I could ride my bike around town. I originally told them I was going to the arcade in town, but really, I wanted to see the quarry where Crystal died. I rode my bike there, which took about a half hour, and when I arrived, the place was empty. Caution tape was stretched between some thin wooden poles to mark where I guess Crystal fell. I got off my bike and walked over to the edge of the quarry, tearing the caution tape down. Bruce Wayne wouldn't let caution tape stop his investigation, so it wouldn't stop mine, either.

I looked over the edge of the quarry and saw police-markers at the bottom, where I imagine Crystal's body was found. I got off my stomach, dusted myself off and looked around the area. No houses, no streetlights, only spotlights for the workers during hours of operation. Fences, sure, but those are easily climbable. I noted a large hole in the fence, and when I examined it, it reminded me of the time dad and I cut some fencing for the garden using his bolt cutter. There were even little pieces of the fence in the dirt and grass, from where whoever cut the fence went through. I also noticed a pay phone nearby that had a cut cable connecting the handset to the actual coin-operated phone part.

I returned to the edge of the quarry and guessed that the drop was about sixty feet, thinking that ten of my old mans could fit in the hole, standing on each other's shoulders. When I got home, I did some research and found that the quarry produced gneiss, which is blueish-gray and was mostly used as a building stone for the old churches and stores in town. Nowadays, the company who runs the quarry provides the stone for repairs, as well as for the school system. Why the school would need so much blue rock, I don't know, but apparently that's the case.

Sunday morning, I asked my dad why the quarry would send so much rock to the school, and he laughed. "They don't just dig rocks, kiddo, they do repairs and upgrades and updates, stuff like that, like a construction site."

"Oh," I said, the Captain Crunch tearing at the roof of my mouth in that oddly satisfying way.

"Why so curious about the quarry, anyway?" I saw him share a look with my mom when he asked.

I shrugged. "I never knew what it was until that girl was found there. Kids at school were talking about it, I guess."

That day, mom and dad took me to lunch, then to the local toy store, where I bought a Batman utility belt with functional pouches and pockets and even a plastic flashlight complete with Bat-signal design. That night, when we got home, I went up to my room and filled the pouches and pockets with various items: stink bombs from when me and Tommy Doyle wasted our allowance at the magic store, black snake fireworks, which are essentially just a black disc until lit on fire, when they produce a ton of smoke, and grow into an ashy snake-looking thing, paper clips, matches, a lighter, batteries for the flashlight, plyers; and finally, my replica batarang dad got me for Christmas two years ago.

I was surprised it all fit in the belt, which was a little too big for me, but it looked awesome. I put the belt on the last loop, but it still was too big, so before leaving for school, I asked my mom to find a way to make it tighter, and when I got home, she folded and sewed the belt tighter, so when I put it on the last hole to fasten it, it fit perfectly. That night, I put all the items into the pockets and grabbed a black towel from the laundry room and placed it over my shoulders in front of the mirror. I looked awesome. I just wish I had the cowl to go with the towel-cape.

On Tuesday, principal Himbry called me into his office. I hadn't done anything bad in a little while, so I had no idea why I'd be in trouble. When I got to his office, he was sitting behind his desk, looking at my folder. "Why were you at the quarry the other night?"

Worried, I lied and told him I wasn't.

"Don't lie, Charlie, I know you were there, I know lots of things," he said, his voice getting quiet.

In that moment, I don't know what it was, but I kept up the lie. "I was at home, sir, I don't know what you're asking me about."

"Stop lying!" He pounded his fist on the desk, causing me to jump. Seeing how scared I was, his voice became softer. "Charlie, I'm worried about you. You shouldn't go to the quarry, you're just a kid. Think of what happened to poor Crystal."

"The girl you were touching outside the gym that day," I said, suddenly feeling more bold.

Principal Himbry just stared at me. "You may go, Charlie."

I got up and left his office. He stared at me as I went, and I felt a sudden chill go down my back as I turned and left.

That evening, I returned to the quarry with my utility belt. I had my backpack with me, too, filled with snacks, ziplock bags; and other items I thought would be helpful as I looked for "clues." The police hadn't been back to the area in a while, and the caution tape had been ripped down since I had been there last. The markers where Crystal's body was found were still at the bottom of the quarry, and I decided I'd climb down and get a closer look.

I noticed some movement in the trees that lined the quarry, but didn't think much of it at the time, thinking a deer or bear might've been nearby. I was far enough away that it didn't make an impact on what I was doing, "gathering clues," as it were. When I shined my light on the treeline, there was nothing there.

As the last bits of sunlight faded, I made it down to the markers, and turned on my flashlight. It projected the bat signal, which wasn't super helpful, but looked awesome nonetheless. I looked around, then looked up at the top of the quarry, thinking that it looked higher than sixty feet. A wave of dizziness hit me and I ran through what I thought might have happened the night Crystal went over the edge of the quarry. At first I had a hard time visualizing and staying focused on the task at hand, but then I remembered *The Long Halloween* and *Gotham by Gaslight*, my two favorite Batman stories, and started analyzing things that made sense to my fifth-grade mind.

How could she just fall over the edge like that?

Why would she be here?

Did the police find a bike or scooter or anything? We're a half hour bike ride outside town.

What girl likes to play at a dirty old quarry?

I didn't have any answers for these questions, but they were the ones that ran through my head all night, lying in bed. After school the next day, I rode my bike to Crystal's house (I found her address using the phone book) and knocked on the door. When no one answered, I decided to look around the property a bit. There were no cars in the driveway, and no lights on in the house at all.

Going around the side of the house, I spotted what had to be Crystal's bike, which was covered in Power Rangers stickers. I walked over to it and ran my hands along the handlebars, thinking that she'd never ride it ever again. A wave of sadness hit me and I decided to look through the windows into the house, and when I did, I saw pictures of Crystal and her parents on a mantle, along with Crystal and other people, other family, I suppose. She was an only child, like me, with a beaming smile, and that ever-present ponytail.

Her Power Rangers sweatshirt lay draped over the arm of the couch. I imagined that she came home from school and changed her clothes, leaving it there, and her parents didn't have the heart to move it or put it in the wash. That made me sad, too, thinking about what her parents were going through. I got back on my bike and rode home thinking about her parents and her and the lifeless sweatshirt.

While sitting in my room that night, making note of the findings from the quarry and Crystal's house, I heard a strange tweet sound from outside. I stood up and walked over to my window, expecting to see a bird on the fence that lined our property, but when I looked, I saw a shadowy figure of a large man looking up at my window. Scared by this, I backed away slowly, closing the window in the process. I returned to my desk a moment, then ran to my parents' room and told them what I saw.

Dad went outside and checked, but found nothing. I was worried they would think I was nuts or making things up, so I apologized and told them I must have been tired or something. Dad tucked me into bed, looked over my utility belt and said he'd have to get me a mask to go with it.

"It's called a *cowl*, dad," I corrected.

"Ah, yes, a *cowl*, sorry, Batman."

"Goodnight, daddy," I said as he closed the door. Not long after that, I dozed off and dreamt of Crystal standing on the edge of the quarry. I saw her fall and watched as her body broke when she slammed into the hard rock below.

In the dream, none of the things I found at the scene added up, just as they didn't in real life. The hole in the fence. Her bike being at home. The next day, I was at school and unable to focus on any of the material my teacher was covering, and instead, I was doodling in my notebook various ideas as they related to Crystal at the quarry and why she would've been there. The shadowy figure outside my house the night before wasn't lost on me either, and when I thought about people who matched the size and shape of that shadow, there was only one obvious answer - principal Himbry.

I went to his office and asked his secretary for an appointment, but he was booked solid for the day. I looked in the window to his office and saw two policemen in there with him. He looked anxious and sweaty, but he usually looked like that, so I wasn't totally sure anything was up. He saw me staring at him from the office and nodded to me.

After school, I decided to talk to Crystal's parents, so using the same phone book from before, I called. This time, they were home. I told them I was a friend of Crystal's and asked if it was okay if I came by to see them and talk to them. Probably because I was only a dorky fifth grader, they agreed, and over I went, meeting her parents for the first time and introducing myself, "I'm Charlie, I'm in fifth grade, but Crystal and I would talk in school. I hope it's okay that I'm here."

Crystal's mom was pretty and kind, her eyes sad and watery. "Of course it is. A friend of Crystal is a friend of ours, come in."

Crystal's mom showed me to the living room, the room I saw through the window, and I took note of the photos on the mantle and the others on the wall, now that I was closer to them. I saw the sweatshirt on the couch. Crystal's dad was upstairs, I learned, in her room.

"I'm really sorry to come by like this, I just wanted to introduce myself and tell you I missed her," I said, half lying.

"Crystal didn't have too many friends, especially not ones that came over. She spent most of her time in her room, reading comics and watching TV."

"Me too, that's why we became friends, I guess. I'm a big Batman fan and she loved the Power Rangers, so we'd talk about that," I said, looking at the sweatshirt.

"That was her favorite. Showed up one day on the porch as a birthday present for her out of the blue. She said it was from someone at school, was that you?"

I shook my head. "Nope, not me."

Someone from school? A girl with no friends suddenly getting gifts from someone from school? Not likely.

"She was in the Power Ranger fan club, did you know that? Billy, the blue one, he was her favorite," Crystal's mom said, holding the sweatshirt.

"I'm really sorry," I said, rising. "I won't bother you anymore, I just wanted to tell you I'm sorry and if you need anything, my name is Charlie Van Sciver. Here's my phone number."

I scribbled my number down on a piece of paper and slipped it to Crystal's mom. She smiled and thanked me. Before I left, she gave me the hardest hug anyone's ever given me in my life.

While riding my bike home, a car was behind me most of the time, following just far enough away not to be noticed, unless you're paying attention. A brown car. Principal Himbry's car, always in the school lot with a space marked "Reserved For Principal." When I got a block from my house, he drove by slowly, and though I couldn't see into the driver's side window of his car, I knew he was watching me.

That weekend, I decided to spy on principal Himbry, sort of in retaliation for him being outside my house and for following me home from Crystal's, but also because he needed to pay for having something to do with Crystal's death. It was clear to me. These kinds of things don't just happen. Crystal didn't just fall into the quarry. There's literally no reason why she would have been there. Someone did this to her and to me, that someone is principal Himbry. I packed my dad's old tape recorder, along with two ninety-minute cassette tapes.

Again using the trusty phone book, I found his house in the Palisades and when I got there, he wasn't home. The utility belt around my waist was filled with my tools, and I had a gameplan. If he was going to be home, I was going to force him to confess about what happened with Crystal. If he wasn't, I was going to snoop around his house looking for clues. Either way, I was dead-set on Himbry going to jail. I waited until my parents were asleep before sneaking out of the house around eleven at night.

Before I left, I grabbed my old ski mask from the time dad and I took a boy's trip to Vermont for some snowy fun, and a black bed sheet from the linen closet. Tying the sheet into a cape and cutting the bottom off, I slipped it over my shoulders. The mask went on easily. As I rode my bike in the darkness, I was worried the cape would get snagged in the spokes of my bike, so I tied it around my waist, creating almost a parachute effect while I was riding, but nevertheless, it worked.

I unhooked my cape from my waist and let it fall to my feet. In the moonlight, I must have looked pretty cool. Or maybe I looked like a scrawny kid with a ski mask and a ripped bed sheet tied around his neck and shoulders, I don't really know. Noting that Himbry's car wasn't in his driveway, I stepped up to the front door of the large house and checked the knob. Locked. I took the paper clips from my utility belt and started fidgeting with the lock. This always looked easy in movies and comics, but was surprisingly difficult in reality. After a while, I gave up and slipped around the side of the house, the late night sounds of cicadas and crickets pushing me onward.

Eventually, I found an open window and shimmied in. I landed hard on a large wooden case under the window, and hurt my back, but it didn't stop me. *How many times has the Caped Crusader been hurt on the job and continued on?*

I clicked my flashlight on, and the image of the bat signal extended outward. I made my way around the house, carefully stepping to avoid making any noise, should Himbry actually be home, despite the fact his car was nowhere to be found. I made a note of the photos on the wall, most of Himbry himself at various school functions, but some of an older woman who bared a striking resemblance to our fair principal. I figured it must be his mother, and turned a corner into the foyer of the house, and started upstairs.

Once upstairs, I tried various doorknobs, but most were suspiciously locked. Eventually, I came to one that wasn't and when I opened it, I was met with a large bedroom. As I walked around, the mask started feeling constricting so I slid it up, revealing the lower part of my nose and the entirety of my mouth. The room itself smelled musty, as though no fresh air had ever entered the room. The walls were empty, with the exception of the windows, which were blacked out somehow.

I ran my finger along the windowsill, which was covered in dust. I stared at the dust on my finger blew it off. I had seen people in movies do that a million times, so it came natural. There was something else tinged with the smell of musty air. Something bitter in the air. I opened the closet door and saw it was empty, except for a metal box with a lock on it. I took out another paper clip and attempted to pick the lock, and after a moment, it worked.

I opened the box slowly, and didn't recognize the contents. A pink plastic ball with two leather straps and a belt loop connected to it. A riding crop like horseback riders use. A pair of bells connected to alligator clips, like the kind dad and I used when we installed an electrical socket last summer.

I put the items back in the box, closed it and locked it again. Still crouching down, I turned and looked around the room again. Something under the bed caught my eye, and as I crawled closer, I aimed the light at it. A black converse sneaker. I pulled it out and something behind it, crumpled in a pile fell forward. I pulled it out: green gym shorts and a pair of pink, girls underwear.

Oh my god ...

Suddenly, I heard a car door slam. Rising quickly and not realizing I left the shorts, underwear, and sneaker on the floor, I rushed to the stairs and started down, but as I got to the landing, the front door opened, and principal Himbry came stumbling in. He moved carefully, bracing himself along the wall, and didn't seem to notice me as he headed toward the kitchen. I stood there, on the landing of the steps, watching him, my mask still pulled up a bit so I could breathe easier.

I crept down the stairs and watched him. He bobbed back and forth in the kitchen, drinking orange juice directly from the bottle the way my mom always scolded me not to. I kept my hand on my flashlight and the other on the doorframe to the kitchen. He looked over at the open window in the living room that I fell through. The box had moved a bit from me falling on it, and the carpet was bunched up from my landing.

I watched him carefully as he examined the carpet, then the box. Without warning, he turned and spotted me, and began laughing. "Who's that? What the fuck are you wearing?"

It was the first time I heard an adult that wasn't my dad curse. I didn't say anything. My body was shaking due to a combination of fright and adrenaline. My hand gripped the flashlight tighter.

"Halloween isn't for a few more months, bud," he said, stumbling toward me.

"Back off," I said, pulling out the flashlight and shining it in his face. Blinded, he stumbled back, tripping over the bunched-up carpet.

He groaned on the ground, and I walked closer to him, my hand on the batarang on my belt. "Principal Himbry, what did you do to Crystal?" Secretly, I pressed the "Record" and "Play" buttons on the tape recorder.

He started laughing. "What're you talkin' about? Who do you think you are?"

"I saw the things in the box. I found her clothes under your bed. What did you do, principal Himbry?" I couldn't believe the words coming out of my mouth. It was like I was possessed by the spirit of vengeance, that I actually was Batman in that moment. I felt strong. I felt a rush of power that washed away the nerves, but not the fear. The fear remained. While the tape recorder ran, I gripped the batarang tighter.

"You wouldn't understand. Crystal was my special little thing, my sweet girl," he said. "You don't understand anything, who do you think you are, I can't even believe you!"

"I am justice, principal Himbry. You're going to jail for what you did to her."

I stepped away from him and toward the front door. Without warning, he rushed at me, and with reflexes that I never had before, nor since, I released the batarang in one fluid motion. It caught him directly in the shoulder and sent him flying backwards, crashing into a glass coffee table.

Running from his home, I found a gas station up the road and called the police. I stayed in the shadows and watched as they searched principal Himbry's home. I saw them carry the batarang out in a plastic bag. Moving quickly and silently, I placed the tape from my recorder on the dashboard of an open police car.

A week or so later, I was watching the news with my parents, and they played the tape from my confrontation with principal Himbry. The news seemed mystified as to who the person on the tape was, but when I listened to it, all I heard was my own voice. When the news played the recording back, though, my voice was deep and guttural. My parents were amazed by the recording.

The voice simply wasn't mine. I had never heard it before that evening watching the news. The closest was while reading comics, the voices I'd hear for the heroes in my head, most specifically, for the caped crusader himself. Masking his identity by using a different voice, something more primal and ugly than what he normally sounded like. Something elemental, almost spiritual. The voice of vengeance itself.

The newspaper in town and even in New York City reported on the mysterious vigilante who apprehended the child-murdering principal. Himbry didn't have a clear memory of what had happened the night I broke into his house, only saying that a tall, dark figure entered his home and made him confess.

I've kept this secret for a long time, even as I grew up and became a detective in town. I don't know what principal Himbry saw in me that night. Maybe it actually *was* the spirit of vengeance coming through me. Maybe my mantra of *what would Batman do?* finally brought it out in me?

Whatever the reason, I'm glad it did.

The Dunderbergs

The prom was in full swing by the time Terry Hamlin had popped a second Vicodin with his friends in the cramped bathroom of the Hudson 'Ho cruise ship. Terry and his friends found no end of enjoyment that the company had the word "Ho" in it. The boat itself was enormous, probably more of a yacht, but Terry, a solid C+ student all throughout his high school career (and middle school, and elementary school) wasn't up on his boat classifications, so to him, the yacht was just "a boat." He wasn't a bad kid, just not bright. Sure, he enjoyed beers with his buddies, the occasional illegal substance (like the pills) and had made his way through most of the cheerleading squad, but he wasn't a bully, and tried hard to learn, even though he just couldn't quite get there. Senior year, he was named captain of the team. To celebrate, his parents took him to Applebee's for dinner.

Terry's doctor had proposed the idea that maybe he had a learning disability. This was back in elementary school, and Mr. and Mrs. Hamlin didn't want to hear any of it. "Not my son, he's no retard," Mrs. Hamlin said, dismissing the potential diagnosis of her son. Terry sat there, quietly, unable to speak for himself, since he knew that if he did, his dad would be sure to "correct his behavior" later that evening, typically with a belt. Terry learned early on to keep quiet and not cross his parents, so by the time he got to middle school, the "correcting" stopped and he was a compliant, "good" boy.

Terry had gotten the painkillers from his doctor after suffering an injury on the lacrosse field, which was his only way of getting into college. During the big game against John Philips Sousa two months prior, Terry had taken a hit that ended up nearly tearing his knee apart. Thankfully, after a month of physical therapy and strengthening, his knee was just about back to normal, even though he missed the last two months of the season, it was more important to recover and make sure his scholarship wasn't in jeopardy. *There's no way I'm missing out on college over my stupid knee*, Terry kept in mind while he worked harder than ever before building up the strength in his knee.

The Patriot is what the yacht was named, and it was the largest in Hudson 'Ho's cruise line. A pristine white pearl color, but adorned with red, white and blue bunting for celebrations like the Resting Hollow High School prom, the Patriot cast a stark contrast in the night as it floated down the river towards New York City. The yacht had started in town, as part of the deal with the high school, and the kids were slated to port in Manhattan around eleven at night, with buses provided to take them to the Hyatt Times Square, before being bussed back to town the following afternoon. All in all, a pretty swaggy prom.

Terry, whacked out of his mind, the pills starting to kick in, stumbled out onto the bow of the yacht and saw the captain standing, watching the mountains as they moved slowly down the Hudson River, looking like solid black cutouts against a dark blue-black sky.

"You okay, son?"

Terry nodded, leaning against the rail beside the captain. "What're you looking at, sir?"

He was always respectful, much more than a lot of other kids his age. Adults liked that about him. The captain immediately clocked that Terry was drunk or stoned or whatever, but he figured the kid had worked hard all year and looked like an athlete, so why give the kid trouble?

"The mountains. We're supposed to salute them when we go past," the captain said.

"Salute them? Why?"

"Old superstition. Goblins in the mountains, Dunderbergs they called 'em, supposedly they watch all the ships that go by, and if a captain doesn't salute, they get pissed," the captain says, with a chuckle. "Crazy stuff people used to believe, right?"

The captain started back toward the control room of the yacht. "Hey, aren't you gonna' salute 'em?" Terry called after him.

The captain just laughed and ducked back into the ship. Terry turned toward the mountains and stared into the darkness. The engine hummed, and the water splashed as the yacht cut through it. Turning slowly, Terry went back into the common area of the yacht, where the DJ and dancing was hitting a peak.

***

A couple hours later, Terry and his friends were dancing to "Jump Around" by House of Pain, a "classic," as they called it when they used it to get hyped up for a game. As they partied and jumped, literally, around the dance floor, two of Terry's friends suddenly fell over. Laughing, Terry helped them up, but as he did so, the boat pitched to the left and more kids fell over, screaming.

The lights in the room suddenly clicked over to red, and the DJ's sound cut out. A click and squeal of a radio system suddenly came to life with a crackle. "Ladies and gentlemen, stay calm, we have grazed a small rock formation along the side of the ship, but we've cleared it. We apologize for the sudden shift," Terry recognized the voice as the captain while he continued to help kids and some teachers back to their feet.

"What about the power?" Terry said, looking around, the entire boat now bathed in red light.

Without warning, the boat shifted again, knocking the DJ booth over, sending speakers and other equipment flying. More kids and teachers hit the deck, and Terry found himself sliding along the floor, grabbing at anything to steady himself. An ungodly metal screaming erupted from the boat and Terry struggled, the sound deafening. He watched as everyone around him tried scrambling to their feet, only for the boat to rock again, knocking them over.

Terry slowly braced himself against the wall and stood up, the boat still being rocked. He waited for the captain to come back over the radio with instructions, but it never happened. He looked around for his friends, but they were missing in the red of the ship and the throngs of people thrown all over. He walked passed a girl screaming on the floor, her arm broken, hyperextended in an unnatural way. Two teachers were tending to her, but she was inconsolable.

The principal stood in the center of the crowd, trying to calm everyone down, but people scattered all over the yacht, screaming and shoving each other. Terry walked passed the principal out onto the deck, making his way to the control room of the yacht. Once there, he banged on the door, but it wouldn't budge. He peered through the small window on the door, and saw sparks, smoke and fire inside. He couldn't see any of the crew, though.

"Captain?" Terry shouted, still pounding on the door.

Suddenly, more screaming, as something on the side of the port side of the boat was flung overboard. Terry walked to the left side and watched as a couple of his classmates, though the boat was perfectly still and silently coasting along the water, were tossed overboard, as though someone was throwing them. Confused, Terry looked toward the screaming. On the dance floor were a group of four foot tall figures that Terry initially thought were kids on their knees, but when he noticed their legs were bent at the wrong angle and their arms stretched the lengths of their entire bodies, this thought vanished from his mind.

One of the creatures grabbed the principal, lifted him above his head and twisted the principal's body the way one wrings out a towel. The sickening snap of bones was punctuated by an explosion of blood from the principal's mouth. With that, the creature lobbed the principal overboard, his body splashing into the dark water. It was then that Terry was able to get a good look at it: sinewy muscles pulsed under dark translucent flesh. Their eyes were remarkably bright, moving across the crowd of teenagers and chaperones, darting from person to person. The creature's bald head had two small holes on the side where a human's ears would be. There was a sheen of wetness on the creature's nude body.

More followed similar fates to the principal. Terry watched as classmates were torn apart, sometimes limb from limb, and tossed overboard. Terry ran to the back of the yacht, where he remembered one of the lifeboats was, and was happy to see some of his classmates and teachers had already climbed on. Suddenly, one of the creatures landed on the lifeboat, tearing it from its moorings, crashing it into the side of the yacht, where most of the students fell out, into the water. Eventually, the lifeboat snapped free, crashing into the people below, exploding into pieces of wood, metal and glass, and crushing those who spilled off the lifeboat.

An emergency horn started sounding on the yacht as Terry ran toward the front of the boat, searching for another lifeboat. Once there, he saw that during the confusion, the Patriot had taken on a course headed directly toward the side of a cliff. Terry paused and braced himself for impact. He thought of his parents. He thought of his friends. He thought of the game against Meadowbrook where he scored five goals. The Vicodin had worn off due to the overwhelming amount of fear and adrenaline coursing through his veins.

He heard steps behind him. When he turned, he was face to face with one of the creatures. Shaking, he closed his eyes and prepared to be ripped apart. Remembering what the captain said earlier, out of desperation, Terry saluted the creature.

His eyes closed, Terry waited for what seemed like an eternity. When he opened them, the creature was gone. He looked around the boat, at the classmates and teachers still alive and safe, and sighed. The goblins were gone, and everyone who was still on the boat was okay.

If only Terry could've steered the Patriot away from the cliff wall.

The Rainbow Prism

The smell of pine cleaner filled the room as Craig stared out the window. His mother, Deliah, was scrubbing the floors, cleaning up an accident Craig had earlier that morning, because he wasn't let out of his room in time to make it down the hall to the bathroom. The pain in his stomach became a dull roar after about forty minutes of holding in his bowel movement. He had pounded on the door, and heard the locks on the outside shake and slam against it, but his mother never came.

"You're a disgusting little piggy," Deliah said. "You should be cleaning this up, not me."

"I'm sorry, mother," Craig said, though he wasn't really sorry. At fourteen years of age, Craig hadn't been sorry for much, and didn't really understand what the concept meant. He hadn't been given the opportunity to make many mistakes, so the concept of being sorry for something was a bit foreign to him.

Sometimes Deliah would scold him for eating his soup too fast, and he would absent-mindedly tell her he was sorry, but after nearly a full day of not eating, Craig was more focused on getting something in his stomach than with his mother's feelings of decorum.

The room Craig lived in didn't have much of note. About six months after the accident on the floor, a toilet was installed in the corner of the room, next to a wooden shelf that was empty with the exception of a picture of Deliah in her 20's, sitting on the hood of a red car and wearing sunglasses, blowing a kiss to the person taking the picture. There was a blue rubber ball, which Craig would sometimes bounce against the wall, but for the most part, went ignored. The bed, which sat underneath the primary source of Craig's entertainment, the window, featured a sheet and a solitary pillow.

The window looked out over the town. Craig would often find himself staring at the people coming and going in and out of Resting Hollow, a town he never walked himself, filled with air he'd never breathed, and sunlight he never felt, with the exception of the times the sun beamed through the window, but even then it felt like artificial sun, reflected through the window provided by his mother, not anything true.

Even though he could never open it, the window was the only connection to the outside world Craig had. Once, when he was ten, he tried to smash it open with the ball, but it didn't work. When Deliah came in, having heard the noise during one of her parties downstairs, she slapped Craig's face and pinched him so hard between his legs that blood appeared every time he peed. At the time, he peed in the corner of the room, in a ceramic coffee cup, but that was where the toilet was now. Craig preferred the toilet because it meant less reliance on his mother. He never made a bowel movement in the coffee cup solely because it wasn't practical, the cup was small, and though he thought about it, he just couldn't figure out exactly how to make it work.

Craig wondered if the toilet could be taken apart and used to smash the window. He decided against it, remembering the pain that surged through his body as his mother gripped his member between her fingers. That sharp, electric pain that felt like it could instantly kill him, but didn't. He wish it had. Many times, in bed, at night, he prayed he wouldn't wake up, because, even though he didn't know much about the world outside, only what Deliah had told him (*the air is filled with chemicals and only a few can breathe it without being sick*) Craig knew that these things weren't true and that he wouldn't get to see other people up close. Only Deliah. Only his mother.

It was during one of these nightly prayers for his own demise that Craig eventually drifted off to sleep. In his dreams, he saw colors he hadn't seen in person, he saw people up close in a way his window couldn't provide, and he stood in a green field, the soft prickle-feeling of cool grass beneath his feet. He breathed the air deeply, and felt his lungs filling with the scent of the outside world, which he imagined to smell fragrant with flowers and warmth from the sun.

Upon waking the next morning, Craig saw remnants of the colors from his dream. At first, the colors seemed to dance on the wall opposite his bed, about three feet from the shelf with the picture on it. Craig rose and walked to the wall, his fingers slipping into the colorful dancing. He let his fingers dance and glide along the wall, the colors flitting between his fingers, with almost a life of their own. For the first time in a long time, Craig smiled.

The familiar sound of keys jingling forced Craig back to his bed. As the door opened, the colors on the wall vanished, which scared Craig a bit, but he knew that if he mentioned what scared him, Deliah wouldn't understand and would scold him. Even though Craig was young, he knew that the goal every time Deliah entered his room was to get her out of there as quickly as possible, with the lowest possible outcome of bodily and/or emotional harm.

When his mother entered the room, she had a tray of toast, jam and half a sliced orange for him. There was a tall glass of water, too, which Craig finished quickly. While he ate, he kept his eyes locked on the spot where the colors danced previously. He kept his eyes there while Deliah's hands disappeared under the covers and up his legs and she began to disrobe.

That evening, Craig waited, his eyes locked on the spot on the wall. He had eaten lunch (half a tuna sandwich, a hardboiled egg and a glass of lemonade, the same as every day of his life) with Deliah a short while earlier and because she had a "hot date" with a doctor from town, she was leaving Craig alone for the night. As Craig thought about his mother on a date with a doctor (a profession he knew about but had no experience with), the colors reformed on the wall and he stepped closer to them. He looked at the window, then back to the colors, trying to figure out exactly where the colors had come from. Perhaps light reflecting from the sun or moon catching the window at a certain angle? Maybe the stars or clouds? Whatever the case was, Craig was glad for the new arrival in his room.

As time progressed, Craig spent time studying the colors. When he tried to touch them, they would shift and dance around his fingers, almost alive. He dreamed of the colors. Always, he was bathed in them, his clothing vanishing in darkness, and replaced with living colors crawling all over his skin, tickling him and feeling cool against his bare skin.

After one particularly vivid dream where the colors pulsed and spoke to him in a language he didn't understand, Craig awoke to the sun piercing through the window at an intensity he never experienced before. As though he were drifting, Craig found himself walking toward the colors on the wall, which seemed to grow and expand, the closer he got, until eventually, the colors vibrated and danced, the size of his own body, as though his shadow had been replaced with pure, vivid color. Craig reached toward the rainbow on the wall, and when he touched it, he found himself in the place he dreamed of so many times. The field. The grass. The color swirling all over and through his flesh. He smiled as the itch and burn of the color invaded his being.

About the Author

Robert P. Ottone is an author, teacher, and cigar enthusiast from East Islip, New York. He delights in the creepy.

About the Publisher

Spooky House is a small indie imprint dedicated to publishing lo-fi horror, speculative science fiction, and more.

Printed in the USA
CPSIA information can be obtained
at www.ICGtesting.com
LVHW041125261024
794885LV00009B/453